Dance Divas

Airin Emery

Published by Lechner Syndications

www.lechnersyndications.com

Copyright © 2013 Airin Emery

ISBN 13: 978-1-927794-01-2

"Great dancers are not great because of their technique, they are great because of their passion."

— Martha Graham

.

CONTENTS

1   New Season   Pg # 1

2   Choreography   Pg # 7

3   New Friends   Pg # 13

4   The Pyramid   Pg # 17

5   Old Friends, New Enemies   Pg # 23

6   Measuring Up   Pg # 31

7   Solos   Pg # 35

8   First Competition   Pg # 45

9   Dance, Sleep, Repeat   Pg # 55

10 Trophy Life   Pg # 59

11   Fatigue, Fears & Friends   Pg # 65

12 Co Dance   Pg # 73

13 Wardrobe Malfunction   Pg # 81

14 Weak Pulse   Pg # 87

15 Truth   Pg # 93

16 Tremaine   Pg # 99

17 Co Dance Nationals   Pg # 101

18 Finale   Pg # 105

19 Cheers   Pg # 113

20 New Chapter   Pg # 115

AIRIN EMERY

CHAPTER 1: NEW SEASON

"Do you want some lipstick? I have pink bubblegum and crimson red in my purse, honey," Amanda Little says. Kelsi sits in the passenger's seat and looks out the window. Her hair is slicked back in a tight bun. She has no make-up on and is wearing a plain black-hooded sweatshirt with "NYCB" embroidered across the chest.

"No thanks. I'm fine," Kelsi says.

"Are you sure? You could use a bit of color. You don't want your friends thinking you've completely changed over one summer," Amanda replies.

But I have. I have changed.

"No mom, I'm fine thanks."

"Excited for a jazz class today after doing nothing but ballet for months?"

Not really. Oddly enough.

"Yeah. It will be good to let loose a bit."

I wonder if I'll remember everything.

"I bet your friends are excited. Avelyn must be dying to see you."

Kelsi nods. "I know. I have so much to tell her."

The car pulls up outside a small dance studio. Two girls stand outside and talk.

"Hey, there's one of the three amigos."

Bailey, tall and muscular, flips her long auburn hair back as she laughs. She is dressed in electric blue T & A shorts and a Hollister burnout T-shirt, with a plaid shirt wrapped around her waist.

Amanda parks and looks at the girls. "Who's that with Bailey?"

Kelsi looks up and stares at them. Beside Bailey is a petite brunette with serious dark eyes. She is dressed to perfection in pure white, right down to the matching boots and purse with a gold and white dance bag. She looks around constantly to see who is noticing her.

"I've seen her around school. I think her name's Hilary." Kelsi says.

"Huh. Wonder if she's starting here?"

"I don't know."

Kelsi watches the girls laugh and make silly faces at one another. She walks up unnoticed.

I see things have changed.

* * * * * * * * * * * * * * * * * * *

Sabine stands in a large kitchen and munches on a bag of chips. She is petite and tanned with sandy blonde, chin length hair and almond-shaped green eyes. Her tiny frame is slightly hunched forward – bad posture, just a lack of confidence.

"Sabine!" Mrs. Howser yells as she walks into the room. "You know what I said. Carrot sticks or celery only. The last thing we need is for you not to fit into your Lulu shorts or have a roll hanging over. Why, you'd be the laughing stock of the studio for sure! I don't think I could handle that embarrassment. This is your year, remember. You're going to kill the competition."

She takes the bag of chips from Sabine and hands her a carrot instead.

"Think smart."

"Yes, mother." She rolls her eyes and bites into a big carrot.

"Speaking of which, let's go over the game plan."

Mrs. Howser pulls out a large file. She grabs one stack and unfolds the connected papers. They fall down to the ground.

"You added more pages?"

"Yes, but that's beside the point. This is very serious business."

She starts at the top and points to the page.

"I need you to get Miss Donna on board with the plan. Step one, convince her you're the best. Step two, suggest the following competitions which we know you can dominate and win scholarships at. Step three…"

Sabine raises her hand.

Mrs. Howser lifts an eyebrow. "Yes?"

"Are there any steps in there for fun?" Sabine asks.

"What are you talking about? This is all fun. The goal is fun!"

Sabine flashes a fake grin.

"Now, repeat after me. Miss Donna, I really think we should talk about the competition schedule."

She nods to Sabine.

"Miss Donna, I think we should talk about the competition schedule."

"There are a couple of really good ones that can give us some positive PR and help the studio stand out in the community."

"There are some super good ones which can help make us stand out and give us the PR we need to become superstars," Sabine says sarcastically.

"Enthusiasm, Sabine," Mrs. Howser says.

Sabine looks at the clock.

"Uh, mom."

"Sabine, we don't have time."

"Exactly." She points to the clock, "I'm gonna be late."

Mrs. Howser grabs her purse and hurries to the door. "Let's go. You can't be late for your first day."

Sabine slings her dance bag over her shoulder and walks out of the room.

* * * * * * * * * * * * * * * * * *

Water pours out of a faucet in a small bathroom. A pair of green finger- nailed hands splash cold water up to a downturned face. Avelyn turns off the faucet and looks in the mirror. There are bags under her young eyes. Her dark layered hair falls forward into her face. She sighs and grabs an elastic from her wrist and makes a quick ponytail.

I need sleep.

Avelyn opens a make-up bag and pulls out some foundation. She blots a couple dots under her eyes and blends them in.

I hope everything stays the same.

She takes the blush out and uses a large brush to apply some color to her cheeks.

Summer was so long this year.

Avelyn swallows hard as she looks in the mirror and with a shake of her locks, pulls out the hair elastic. Her collarbone protrudes, making her look even thinner than she already is.

What if my bestie no longer likes me? What if she's changed? We've never been apart more than two weeks much less three months. Everything could be different. I'm not ready for 'different'.

The bathroom door swings open. Avelyn quickly grabs a tube of mascara and pretends to be applying more to her lashes. The girl enters a stall and closes the door. Avelyn takes a deep breath and lets it out.

Well, here goes nothing.

She zips up her make-up bag, places it in her dance bag and leaves the bathroom.

* * * * * * * * * * * * * * * * * * *

The girls stretch and pull on glittery leg warmers in the hallway. They chat amongst themselves. Hilary and Bailey giggle by themselves in a corner.

"And then she said that I needed to have my brows waxed," Hilary says.

"Oh, my God, really?" Bailey inquires.

"Yeah. And I was like, Dude, I just had them done. I think you need your back waxed."

"No way, you didn't."

"Yeah, I did. I'm not gonna let some caveman freak tell me I need my brows waxed. As if…"

Hilary throws back her long locks and rolls her eyes. She pouts her lips.

"Oh, Bay, did you remember to bring the pink Uggs you said I could borrow?"

"I said I had to ask my mom, remember? I haven't even worn them yet," Bailey replies.

"They just match my new top so well and I figured it would be cool."

"My mom doesn't like me to loan out my clothes."

"Except, I'm like family. I'm practically your sister. Pretty please." She continues to bat her eyes and act pathetic.

"I'll ask her tonight."

Hilary's attitude does a 360 and she stands up straight, hip out, a look of attitude on her face.

"Good. 'Cuz when I look hot, you are cool by connection."

"That's what friends are for, right?" Bailey says weakly.

Just then, Kelsi walks in. Everyone turns and looks at her. She shyly looks around, then lowers her head. She walks up to Bailey.

"Hey, Bay," Kelsi starts.

Hilary grabs Bailey's arm and spins her around to face her.

"Like I was saying, I'm super jazzed about sharing clothes for school," Hilary says. She pretends to not see Kelsi as she continues by. Everyone is dressed in brightly colored, skin-baring spandex clothing, glittery accessories, and crazy hairstyles. Kelsi's black warm-up pants and hoodie stand out compared to the flashy outfits of the others.

Avelyn bends forward and touches her toes. Kelsi recognizes the hair. She walks toward her and for the first time, and smiles.

"Av," Kelsi says.

Avelyn whips her head up and looks at Kelsi. She nearly falls back when she sees her.

"Kels?"

Kelsi smile widens. Avelyn wraps her arms around her and squeezes tightly.

"Look at you. You're so...you're so...skinny. Did they not feed you there?" Avelyn asks.

Kelsi chuckles. "Nothing but salad. I have so much to tell you."

"Uh, yeah. Like what's up with your hair for starters?"

"It's called a bun." Kelsi models it like Vanna White.

"Think I've heard of that before," Avelyn says jokingly.

"Pretty cool style. Keeps your hair out of your eyes when you turn."

"Really? Why didn't I think of that?" Avelyn's sarcasm is comical. Kelsi can't help but laugh.

"So, how'd you do holding down the fort without me?" Kelsi asks.

"Ya know, there were some rough moments, but basically I rocked it out."

"Wouldn't expect anything less."

Kelsi smiles. She looks at the wall clock in the hall.

"I gotta stretch. Want to join me?"

"But we stretch first thing in class?"

Kelsi ignores her trailing comment and goes to an open doorway. She swings one leg up and extends in a split. Kelsi scoots herself into the doorway and holds the position. Avelyn watches her from a couple feet away.

"New stretch?"

"A lot of the girls did it in New York. It helps your stretch a lot.

You can't cheat this one."

Avelyn nods. She watches Kelsi curiously.

What happened to her? Where's her make-up? And stretching before class? Come on!

Another girl pulls Kelsi's working leg back so she extends past her 180 degree split. Avelyn watches them smile and giggle, jealous.

What if she's more flexible than me now?

Her eyes widen with this sudden realization.

What else is she hiding?

"Get into class or get out of my studio!!!" Miss Donna screams as her smile disappears.

Everyone in the hallway quickly jumps to their feet and rushes into the large dance studio. Hilary and Bailey enter together. Kelsi trails behind with Avelyn. Sabine runs through the front doors of the studio and down the hall, just in time to see Kelsi enter.

Kelsi? What is SHE doing back?

With a look of confusion on her face, Sabine follows behind the others.

CHAPTER 2: CHOREOGRAPHY

"In now, now, now, now, now!" Miss Donna yells. Her spray tan shines in the lights of the studio. "Time is of the essence." The girls all rush in and spread out across the wood dance floor.

Kelsi looks oddly at Miss Donna.

Funny, I don't remember her being so…

Miss Donna adjusts the strap of her bra top accentuating her fake boobs.

"Welcome back, everyone." She smiles. Her bleached teeth look plastic against her darkened skin and almost match her blonde locks.

Kelsi looks around at the studio walls. There are framed photos of Miss Donna as a Rockette on every wall. Each photo has her dressed in a scantily covered outfit and with pounds of make-up on her face. Some have feather boas, others fancy headpieces. Kelsi rolls her shoulders back and circles her neck as she looks around.

"I hope everyone had a good summer vacation. I went to the Caribbean. Anyone else do anything fun for their two weeks off?" Miss Donna asks.

I've been gone for three months.

No one raises their hand.

A small dirty-blonde girl starts, "I saw the American Ballet…"

"Alright, let's get started then." Miss Donna interrupts.

Hi. Remember me? Welcome back, Kelsi?

Miss Donna walks over to a high-tech stereo system and presses a button. Fast-paced techno type music blares.

Kelsi squats in second position, then straightens her legs and bends forward grabbing her ankles to stretch, pulling her sitting-bones up to the ceiling.

Miss Donna jumps around at the front of the room.

"And go!"

She starts a series of jumping jacks, Tae Bo kicks, and hip hop squats. Kelsi shakes her head as she follows along.

What happened to stretch?

Miss Donna and the group continue with cheerleading claps, krumping style movements, and hitch kicks, closer to aerobics than ballet.

Everyone's sequins and dangly hair accessories bounce around as they, too, hop and bounce. Kelsi follows along well, and completes every movement perfectly, but with more grace and agility than the others. Avelyn pushes herself to jump higher and smile wide, even though she is tired. Sabine smiles widely as she skips around and continues to make eye contact by looking at Miss Donna in the mirror. Hilary struggles to keep up but maintains a confident expression throughout. Bailey continues to look over at Hilary, even though she has every step memorized and obviously has much stronger technique.

The song comes to an end.

"How's everyone feeling? Loose and ready to dance?"

Several of the girls speak out excitedly, "Yeah!"

Kelsi looks around; even Avelyn is excited and prances about.

"Time for choreography. Today I'll start setting the choreography for jazz. Over the next three weeks, we'll have this routine, as well as the tap and lyrical dances done. I'll also be deciding who gets the solos this year, so show me your stuff and make me want you."

I have to get a solo this year. Sabine thinks to herself. She shifts back and forth in the center of the room and smiles at Miss Donna. *She'll pick me, I know she will.*

"And last, but certainly not least, we have a new addition this year," Miss Donna says.

The girls all look around at one another, searching for a new face. Kelsi and Avelyn look at Hilary who stands with her hip out and a stuck-up, confident look on her face.

"We're introducing acro to the studio," Miss Donna continues as she speaks through her smiling teeth.

"Acro?" Avelyn says aloud.

"Yes, acro, Avelyn." Miss Donna says, "Other studios are putting back tucks and walkover combinations in their routines and making judges take notice. We're going to up the stakes and add the most complicated and unique tricks to our dances. Things you've never even seen before. Things you never thought were possible."

Sabine swallows hard.

Acro?

"And since you are the advanced group, this class will be mandatory."

Mandatory?

Sabine swallows harder.

"Sounds fun," Avelyn says to Kelsi.

"Yeah. You never know, right?" Kelsi replies.

"Okay, let's start." Miss Donna says as she heads to the stereo, "We're doing a punk rock theme with an 80s remix."

"So cool," Hilary says.

Hilary and Bailey slap hands.

"Let me have Molly, Shawna, Denver and Cecilia line up right here." Miss Donna holds her arm out and the four girls form a line.

"Spread out a bit."

The girls move over and spread out.

"Next line, let's have Harmony, Naomi, Kim and Abby."

Another four girls line up.

"Sabine, on that end," Miss Donna points to one side, "Kelsi, on the other."

Kelsi looks back at Avelyn, unsure as she walks to the outer edge of the next line.

"Bailey and Avelyn, next."

Bailey and Avelyn stand opposite each other splitting center.

"And finally, Hilary, right here downstage center."

Miss Donna points to the center, in front of Bailey and Avelyn. Hilary struts to her place.

"The rest of you split up on either side, off-stage. You'll enter on the second eight count."

The other girls disperse to the sides.

"Everyone, legs second, arms at your side, heads down."

Miss Donna shows off the pose. "And a five, six, seven, eight."

She starts a simple but strong set of four poses which change every two counts. The girls follow along.

Miss Donna claps. "Let me see it."

The girls get into their starting pose.

"Five, six, seven, eight!" Miss Donna yells.

The group hits all the poses. Hilary is a count behind each time. She watches in the mirror to see what's next.

"Alright that was a..." Miss Donna searches for the words. "Let's try it again."

The group starts again. Once more Hilary is behind and watches in the mirror.

Miss Donna tries to smile, "We'll clean it up later."

Kelsi looks over at Avelyn. They both look toward Hilary then back toward one another. "Really?" Kelsi mouths. Avelyn shrugs.

* * * * * * * * * * * * * * * * * *

"So, how was your day?" Mrs. Howser asks as she looks in the rear view mirror of her Escalade. Avelyn and Kelsi look at one another.

"Fine," they both reply at the same time and burst into giggles.

Sabine sits in the front passenger seat. She looks at her mother. "Good, I guess."

"Did you talk with Miss Donna?" she asks in a whisper, glancing to the back at the other two giggling girls.

Sabine shakes her head and glares at her mom. "No."

"What do you have to talk to Miss Donna about?" Avelyn asks.

"Oh, nothing important," Sabine says as she gives her mom a silencing glare.

Mrs. Howser sits upright.

"Tell us about your summer, Kelsi," Sabine follows up.

"It was fun," Kelsi replies. She thinks for a moment to herself and smiles.

It was perfect really.

"What'd you do? Were you like the best dancer there?" Avelyn pries.

Kelsi laughs.

"Not even. The other girls were so amazing. I struggled so much in the beginning but I got better as time went by. I still wasn't even close to the best though. There are some serious ballet girls out there."

"Did you get to do anything else?" Sabine asks.

"Just ballet. Every day." Kelsi smiles.

"Sounds horrible," Avelyn comments.

It was really fun actually.

"Not really." Kelsi says, "The more you do it, the more fun it is, I guess. I really want to do more now."

Mrs. Howser raises an eyebrow.

"Did you meet any cute boys?" Avelyn asks.

Kelsi shakes her head. "No. Pas de deux class is for the next level up. And boys weren't allowed in the girl's dorms so we never got to hang out or anything."

"How about your roommates? Were any of them like really cool, or super mean, or anything? Did you want to go crazy on them like Sookie style or just backstab like The Hills?"

Kelsi just starts to laugh.

"That's the Av I missed. Always in on the drama."

"What? The whole time you were gone I imagined my best friend was on an episode of the latest reality show having the time of her life."

Kelsi half-smiles.

It was a good time. A really good time.

Mrs. Howser interrupts, "So, how's the new routine?"

Sabine smiles, "It's an 80s theme. Totally retro."

"It's alright," Avelyn says.

"Where do you start, Sab?" Mrs. Howser asks.

"Across from Bailey."

"And are you up front, Kelsi?"

"Nope," Kelsi says.

A frown forms across Mrs. Howser's forehead.

"You, Avelyn?"

Avelyn shakes her head.

"Who, then?"

"Hilary," Sabine says.

"Hilary? The new girl?" Mrs. Howser responds.

"I know, right?"

"It is kinda odd," Avelyn says.

"Did you see how off she was with the counts?" Kelsi adds.

The girls nod.

"And how droopy her arms were? She's like a wilting tree," Sabine says.

The three girls giggle.

"Well, I guess I'll have to talk to Miss Donna about that," Mrs. Howser starts. "We wouldn't want anything to make the studio look less than perfect. Because you are, I mean, you all are, perfect."

Mrs. Howser stares straight ahead, focused.

"I wonder if Miss Donna did that to you Kelsi because she's mad," Sabine says.

"Mad?"

"Yeah, I heard her a couple times while you were gone, talk about how she was mad you were missing summer camp."

She's mad at me?

"I don't know, just thinking," Sabine adds.

But she wanted me to go, she said.

"I bet you learned a lot though," Sabine continues.

Kelsi looks out the window in a daze.

"Yeah,...a lot."

Avelyn watches her, concerned.

"I'm sure it was a great experience and well-worth everything," she smiles trying to cheer up the mood.

Was it worth it? Or was it just a waste of time and money? I bet that's what my mom thinks. A waste of money.

Kelsi shakes her head side to side as she mumbles,"Yeah, yeah, it was."

I miss my friends.

Avelyn continues to look at her. Kelsi manages a weak smile.

I want to go back to New York and do ballet. I want things to make sense.

CHAPTER 3: NEW FRIENDS

"And did you see that elbow thing at the end?" Hilary asks.

"Yeah, it was fun...,"she trails off.

"That was super weird. But I still made it look cool."

"Yeah, yeah, you did," Bailey agrees.

"So, do you think I made a good impression on Miss Donna?"

Bailey purses her lips then gently bites on her curled upper lip.

Honestly?

"She put you in the front, didn't she?" Bailey says, avoiding the question.

"Yeah, but I think that had something to do with my dad," Hilary says as she looks at her nails. There's a small chip in one nail. "Oh, no, I have to get that filed right away. Wanna come to the salon with me and have your nails done? You could really use a French mani and pedi."

"Well I have homework, but..."

"Good, it's settled. I'll have my mom call and make us appointments."

Hilary pulls her cell phone out of her Juicy Couture bag.

"Mom...can you book two spots with Georgio today?"

Bailey watches her talk on the phone as they continue to walk down the street after dance.

"No, I need it today. My nail is chipped. I can't be expected to go to school tomorrow in this condition."

Bailey's eyes bug open.

No school because of a nail? Wow. I wish...

"But you said. Can I talk to daddy? Fine then. Thanks. You're the best mom."

Hilary closes her cell phone and places it back in her bag.

"Today at 6:30. Better be there, beotch."

"That's when my family has dinner though."

"I'm sure they won't mind. This is a beauty emergency." Hilary reassures.

Bailey looks down. Hilary puts her hand on Bailey's back.

"Trust me; I used to be like you. Then I learned that you just have to tell your parents what you want and do it. Like my mom, she says I don't need something, then I just say let me talk to daddy. Daddy never says "no" and she knows that. So she just gives me what I want. Works every time."

Hilary smiles proudly. Bailey looks at her unsure.

"You should try it."

"I don't think I could do that," Bailey says.

"Trust me, you can. I know you can. I got the front spot at dance, didn't I?"

"Yeah, so?"

"I bet my dad gave Miss Donna money. Like a lot of money for her 'not for profit' sector of the studio. How else would the new girl get front row center? Works."

"What 'not for profit' sector?"

"The competition team…that we dance on. I told my Dad to get me in so he talks with Miss Donna, makes a donation and I didn't even have to try-out." Hilary whips her hair back and struts as she walks.

There's an awkward moment of silence.

"You look really good in those heels for the dance," Hilary says out of the blue.

Bailey smiles.

"Really?"

Hilary nods.

"To be honest, I'm kinda jealous of you."

"Jealous of me?" Bailey asks. "Why would you be jealous of me?"

"Because you're just so good. I really want to be like you."

Bailey's smile widens even more.

"Think you could help me practice the dance before class?"

Bailey thinks about her schedule.

I have to watch my nephew until 4, and then I have homework before tap and…

"It would just be for a little bit before class," Hilary negotiates.

Bailey just looks at Hilary's pouty lips and frown.

"Pretty please," Hilary pleads.

"Sure," Bailey gives in. "That's what friends are for, right?"

"Great."

Hilary throws her arms around Bailey's neck.

"I'm so glad we're best friends."

"Me too."

Hilary grabs Bailey's hand as they walk.

"Best friends forever," Hilary smiles at Bailey. "Dancin' divas."

"Hey, we have tap tomorrow," Bailey says.

God, I hate tap.

"You're gonna love it. We have so much fun."

"Oh, yay, I love tap." Hilary lies.

I don't even know how to tap.

Hilary's smile turns into a frown. Bailey looks over at her and she quickly smiles again.

What am I going to do?

CHAPTER 4: THE PYRAMID

"Ugh, that was super hard today," Shawna, a thin redhead says as she wipes sweat from her brow. Kelsi tries to hold back a giggle. "What?"

"Nothing," Kelsi says, seriously.

"No, you were laughing at me. What was so funny?"

"Oh, nothing, I was thinking of something funny in my head."

Like how we did 1 ½ hours of just stretch each day and you're whining about twenty minutes of jumping around.

"Not about you at all," Kelsi finishes.

"Oh, okay." Shawna perks up.

Across the room, Bailey nudges Hilary, "Now we have tap."

"I'm so excited!" Hilary fakely says.

Avelyn, Sabine and Kelsi watch the two interact.

"Does it make you guys mad?" Sabine asks.

"No, why would it?" Kelsi replies.

"Because you guys were like the three amigos, now you're just the two amigos. That's not even a thing. I'd want to punch her in the face right now."

"Which one?" Avelyn questions.

"Both of 'em," Sabine says.

Kelsi chuckles. "Wonder if she can tap? Anyone know?" She looks at Avelyn and Sabine. They both shake their heads. "Should be fun."

Sabine stares across the room at Bailey as she pulls on her nude-colored tap heels.

You and me, Bailey. Who can out tap who for the front spot? We shall see.

Sabine's eyes glare, as if in battle.

Hilary ties her black oxford tap shoes. She looks around and notices everyone else has nude tap heels on. She takes in a deep breath of air.

"I'll be back. I have to use the restroom," Hillary says to Bailey.

Hilary stands and walks on her toes across the floor avoiding any sound which might draw attention to her shoes.

Bailey adjusts her shoes and looks up. Kelsi stares at her from the across the room. Their eyes meet.

Kelsi smiles softly. Bailey smiles back. Kelsi raises a hand up and mouths, "Hi." Bailey does the same.

"Tap time, ladies! Mr. Fred is waiting!" Miss Donna yells.

* * * * * * * * * * * * * * * * *

Mr. Fred, a tall, tanned and fit man, claps his hands four times. The group begins a sequence of time steps, pull backs and grab offs. Sabine is in the front, alongside Avelyn. Kelsi taps at the end of the front row. They move through the steps with ease.

Bailey stands in the second row behind Sabine. Hilary is beside on the outer edge. Bailey makes tap look easy. She is smooth and carefree. It's a fun side of her that's suddenly released.

Time step, delayed pull back. Grab off. Pull back right. Grab off. Pull back left.

Bailey happily taps along.

Hilary fights to keep up. She watches Molly's feet in front of her. Hilary crosses her feet around like crazy, trying to just mimic the same movements. She steps on her own toe.

"Owww!"

Hilary shakes her foot and then tries to follow the steps again.

Slow down.

Sabine looks in the mirror and sees Bailey happily tapping behind her. She puts more energy into her next set of steps. Her body bursts with excitement and intensity.

Mr. Fred claps and the dancers stop.

"Very good, very good."

Hilary's brow wrinkles up and she bites her lips.

I hate this.

"Now, let's see some shim sham shimmies."

The girls all perk up and smile.

What's a shim sham...shimmery?

"Four at a time, starting stage right."

Hilary starts to raise her hand to ask a question, then quickly pulls it back into her body.

The girls line up and await their turns. Hilary takes her place in line beside Bailey. The four girls make their way to centre stage. Hilary watches the other girls intensely and mimics their shoulder movements, while in line. Bailey starts onto the floor. Hilary slips behind the person behind her. Then behind another person. She continues to watch.

And one, two, and three…ugh, what is that?

Hilary slips behind the next person in line.

"Go ahead," Hilary whispers. "My shoe's untied."

Across the room, Kelsi watches Hilary move further back in line. She elbows Avelyn and casually nods. Avelyn notices Hilary moving back.

"Guess you got your answer," Avelyn whispers. "Not a tapper."

"Pretty funny, dontcha think?" Kelsi adds.

"Wonder if she'll be in the front of this dance, too?" Avelyn jokes.

"Everyone knows it should be Bailey. She deserves it this year."

They both nod.

It's finally down to the last three dancers, including Hilary to do the shim sham shimmy. She starts off okay, then loses track of the music, so her rhythm is all off. Mr. Fred watches and grimaces a tad, then turns his attention to the other girls in the group.

"Definitely not center," Avelyn says to Kelsi. They both shake their heads.

Mr. Fred turns off the music.

"Now, for competition this year we're going to be a Tap Dogs, Stomp- inspired number. Think regular clothes and crazy tapping in the street."

All the girls look at each other, unsure.

Cecilia raises her hand.

"Yes, Cecilia."

"Will our street clothes have rhinestones and jewels?"

"You'll see."

Cecelia looks puzzled.

"But our studio is known for its always sparkly attire," Harmony argues.

"Don't worry about it. Let's focus on the steps," Mr. Fred says. "Anyway, it starts off a Capella, and then goes into heavy metal music for the chorus. It's tight."

"Can we pull off our regular clothes to reveal a sparkling dream costume underneath, when the heavy metal music starts?"

"Maybe," Mr. Fred says.

"Yes," Harmony slaps hands with Cecilia.

"Watch and learn."

Mr. Fred starts a sequence of rifts, ball heel combinations and stomps. No toe stands or tricks, just pure rhythm. All the girls watch intensely. A couple of them mark along with his movements. Hilary watches and takes a deep breath.

How am I going to pull this one off?

Mr. Fred finishes with a triple turn, followed by a stomp. He pauses for a moment, then relaxes.

"Let me see."

He claps his hands, "Five, six, seven, eight."

The girls start in a flurry of fast feet. Hilary manages the first couple rifts, then gets lost after the first ball heel combination.

What's next?

She watches Sabine's feet, but can't find a spot to even jump in.

I don't know what to do.

Hilary's eyes begin to glaze over. Everything becomes a blur.

What do I do? What do I do?

She freezes up.

Aggghhhhh.

Hilary runs out of the room. "I can't do this." Tears flow from her eyes.

The combination ends and everyone looks around.

"I don't know what that was about," Mr. Fred says. "Moving on, Bailey, that was excellent. You nailed it."

Bailey's face drops; she turns and runs out of the room.

Mr. Fred shakes his head, "What is going on here today?"

No one responds.

"Sabine, you missed the second rift. It had six beats, just not the six I showed - but otherwise good work. Everyone else, let's try it again."

Sabine smiles proudly.

With Bailey out, I'll get the front spot for sure. Thanks, Bay.

Kelsi looks at the door.

What in the world is she thinking? The old Bailey would have never run out of class. The old Bailey would have just kept tapping for hours on end. She loves tap. At least she used to. Maybe things have changed over summer. Maybe she's no longer Bailey.

Kelsi's eyes meet Avelyn's. They share a knowing look.

I know, so weird. They both think.

"And a five, six, seven, eight." Mr. Fred claps.

The girls begin the combination again. Sabine dances feverishly, trying to stand out. She smiles and flirts with herself in the mirror.

* * * * * * * * * * * * * * * * * *

Hilary stands in the bathroom and covers her face. Bailey pats her back.

"It's alright. I'll help you," she says.

Hilary throws her hands away from her face and whips around, sending Bailey's arm flying.

"I don't want help! I want…I want…"

Hilary searches for something to say, she's blank.

"What do you want?" Bailey asks.

"I want to be perfect," Hilary says.

"Perfect? We all want to be perfect. But we have to practice. That's what they always say, right? Practice makes perfect."

Hilary glares in the mirror. Bailey tries to smile and cheer her up. Hilary continues to glare angrily. Bailey takes a step back, unsure what to do.

* * * * * * * * * * * * * * * * * *

The girls are broken up into small groups and work alone in separate corners of the room. Mr. Fred observes.

Miss Donna pops her head into the room.

"How's it going in here?" she says, super enthusiastically.

"Things are coming along nicely," Mr. Fred replies.

"Good. Good. I just wanted to remind everyone that acro starts tomorrow. So, come stretched and ready to bend in all sorts of strange ways, like the Chinese circus. Your choreographer worked for Cirque du Soleil, so be ready for some wild tricks!"

Avelyn's eyes light up.

I love Cirque!

"And," Miss Donna continues, "wear a plain black bodysuit and shorts."

"What?" Molly protests. "A plain bodysuit? How boring!"

"I don't think I even have one," Shawna adds.

"Does it have to be plain?" Harmony asks.

"I'm afraid so. That is what she asked for," Miss Donna replies.

"But that messes with our artistic expression," Naomi reasons. "How can we be expected to show our souls through dance if we're forced to wear the same boring attire as everyone else in the world?"

Miss Donna sighs.

"We wear the same costumes in every competition and we all look the same so there's uniformity. What's the difference?" Kelsi says.

Naomi scowls at her.

"Who let her back?" Naomi mutters under her breath.

"Girls, I expect you to be on your best behavior. Dominique is a highly respected performer and I won't hear of her telling me anyone was out of line." Miss Donna looks around and stares at each of the girls. "Understood?"

The girls all nod.

"I can't hear you."

"Yes, m'am," they all say in unison.

Sabine takes in a deep breath of air.

Circus tricks? I can't even do a cartwheel.

She frowns as she thinks about the following day.

I'll practice. I can do this.

* * * * * * * * * * * * * * * * * *

Sabine preps for a cartwheel on the grass of her back yard. She takes in another deep breath, then goes for it. Her hands touch the ground.

I'm doing it, I'm doing it.

Sabine's feet fall down and she plops onto her butt. She sighs.

I can't do this.

CHAPTER 5: OLD FRIENDS, NEW ENEMIES

Kelsi pulls her booty shorts down, as Harmony and Denver roll the waistbands and lift their shorts up. Kelsi notices their butts popping out of the bottom of their shorts and she shakes her head.

Never in New York.

Avelyn walks up behind Kelsi and sees her tugging on her shorts.

"Got an itch?" Avelyn asks.

"No, these things are so short and they're the longest ones I could find."

Avelyn looks at her puzzled.

"Were they always this short?" Kelsi asks.

"As long as I've been dancing here," Avelyn replies. "Maybe you just grew or something."

"Yeah, maybe."

Miss Donna walks into the large room followed by a lean and fit woman with short jet black hair and delicate features.

"Girls, I'd like you to meet, the one and only, Dominique Rene!" Miss Donna motions to her.

The girls clap. Dominique politely curtsies.

Sabine taps her foot rapidly.

Please don't make me tumble.

"Hello, my name is Dominique Rene and I have been a part of Cirque for ten years."

"Wow!" Avelyn says. She quickly covers her mouth embarrassed her thoughts were out loud.

Dominique chuckles. "Wow, is right. Cirque is unlike anything I had ever been a part of before. And I hope to bring just a little tiny piece of that to you for your competitions."

She looks around at the group.

"Shall we begin?"

The girls all nod, excitedly.

"Well, I'll leave you ladies to it." She smiles at Dominique. "Let me know if you need anything."

Miss Donna waves at the girls and leaves the room.

"Spread out," Dominique says.

The girls all spread out across the floor and face the mirror. Dominique stares at them, serious.

"At the barre, ladies. At the barre."

The girls look confused. They slowly make their way to the barre which wraps around two walls of the studio. Kelsi bites her lip and holds back a smile as she touches the barre with her left hand.

Ah, this feels right.

"Before you can ever begin performing, you must properly stretch."

Yep. I am going to like this class.

"Otherwise, you can become injured. A single injury can end your career as a dancer," Dominique continues.

Several of the girls lean against the barre, and toss their hair back and forth, as they look in the mirror.

Dominique taps the barre.

"Stand up straight."

The girls quickly adjust and stand upright.

Dominique stands in first position. "Eight tendus front, eight side, eight back and side again. Stretch down, port de bras, back and around. Sous sous, turn and repeat."

Kelsi turns out from her hips, her feet automatically shift outward. She lifts her chest, proudly.

The music begins; it's fast and upbeat.

Kelsi's feet work, clean and crisp, through the floor. She holds her upper body strong and still. Dominique walks around and examines all the girls. Harmony slouches as she tries to keep up with the brushes. Denver flexes her feet every time she closes so they lift off the floor. Cecilia has great feet, but her torso wobbles around as she clutches the barre for dear life. Abby and Kim are mediocre. Avelyn has great straight legs and decently-pointed feet. Kelsi shines. Dominique starts inspecting her at the foot level. Kelsi's long toes hit a perfect arch each brush and smoothly come back into first position. Her legs are tightly squeezed together and turned out from the hips. Kelsi's torso is unmoving. Her ribs are closed, and her chin is lifted, showing off a stunning neckline like that of all prima ballerinas. Dominique smiles and continues to walk around. Kelsi sees the smile out of the corner of her eyes, and feels at home for the first time since returning from New York.

Someone who gets it.

* * * * * * * * * * * * * * * * * * *

"Yoga will increase your focus and balance. Pilates will strengthen your core and work your endurance. You're nothing without endurance," Dominique says as she walks around and corrects downward-facing dog positions on all the girls.

"This hurts my ankles," Molly whispers to Shawna.

"It hurts my everything."

"What are we gonna do, morph into animals on stage and hope the judges like it? This is retarded," Molly says.

Kelsi and Avelyn tilt their heads toward Molly and Shawna. They then look at each other, knowingly.

Idiots.

"Breathe in…" Dominique says.

Avelyn and Kelsi breathe in.

"And out. Extend your right leg into the air," she continues.

Everyone lifts their legs up. Kelsi's leg is straight up in the air. Avelyn's leg extends past 180 degrees. Dominique pushes Avelyn's leg even further.

"Excellent stretch."

Avelyn smiles, "Thanks."

Kelsi winks as Dominique walks away. "Show off."

"You're just jealous."

"Heck yeah, I am. I spend a whole summer stretching and I still can't do that."

"But I have noticed it's suddenly a lot easier for you than before."

Kelsi nods. "True. Very true."

They both smile.

* * * * * * * * * * * * * * * * * * *

Avelyn balances on her palms, then presses onto her fingertips. Her legs extend out to the side thighs by resting on her elbows. Everyone else stands and watches.

"Now, straighten your legs," Dominique says.

Avelyn straightens her legs.

Dominique nods, "Good."

Sabine watches, unsure.

Well, this isn't so bad. Circus tricks. Just try. Try Sabine. Do it for…do it for your mom. She's counting on you.

"Now, for the tricky part. You're going to slowly press through your shoulders as you rotate your hips, and push up straight to a handstand," Dominique says.

Avelyn looks up at her, questionably.

"Got it?"

Avelyn nods.

"All in one big sweep."

Avelyn stares forward into the mirror, at herself.

One big sweep.

"One, two, three," Dominique counts.

Avelyn pushes up and then falls.

"Ha, I could do that easy," Hilary comments to Bailey.

"Looks kinda hard," Bailey says.

"Please. That's kindergarten stuff."

Kelsi looks over. Hilary glares at her. She turns back the other way and watches Avelyn shake her arms out and then squat back down.

"That's alright. Try again."

Avelyn resumes her position. She takes in a deep breath, then steadies herself.

One, two, push!

Avelyn pushes straight up with her legs close into a handstand. She starts to wobble, but catches herself by walking around on her hands.

Ahhh.

She kicks down and stands up.

Dominique and several of the girls clap.

That a girl, Av. Kelsi smiles.

Sabine stands and claps, her eyes in a daze.

"Alright, who's next?" Dominique asks.

Sabine steps back, and tries to hide behind Cecilia and Harmony.

"I think Hilary said she'd like to give it a try," Kelsi blurts out. She points to Hilary right behind her.

Hilary's eyes widen.

"Hilary, you'd like to try it out?" Dominique asks.

Everyone turns and looks at Hilary. She gulps, looks side to side then lifts her chin and fakes a confident smile.

"I'd love to."

Dominique motions for her to come forward. Hilary slowly walks forward.

"Um…um…"

Dominique studies her face.

"Just get down like, like…" Dominique looks at Avelyn.

"Avelyn," She replies.

"Like Avelyn."

Hilary looks at Dominique, then at Kelsi and Bailey. Kelsi smiles. Bailey nods for her to try.

"I don't think I can do it," Hilary mumbles.

"I'm sorry, huh?" Dominique asks.

"I don't…."

"What?"

"I don't think I can do it…"

Dominique raises an eyebrow.

"Right now," Hilary continues. "I don't think I can do it now. I'm not feeling so well."

"Oh. Okay," Dominique says. "That's fine. Who else would like to try?"

A couple of girls raise their hands. Hilary walks back to her spot beside Bailey. As she passes Kelsi she grins, "Nice try, amateur."

"Are you okay?" Bailey asks, sincerely worried.

Hilary looks at her with attitude, then suddenly frowns and pouts her lips.

"No, I feel terrible."

She sniffles and pretends to cry. Bailey rubs her back.

"Oh, you poor thing."

Oh, you poor fake is more like it. Kelsi rolls her eyes.

"And for the rest of you, let's pull out some mats and start with front rolls," Dominique says.

A few girls rush over to the corner and grab a couple large blue mats.

Sabine looks around at all the activity. She raises her hand. Dominique points to her.

"Yes?"

"I need to use the restroom."

"Go right ahead. But hurry back. We have lots of fun things to try."
Hurry back, my butt.

* * * * * * * * * * * * * * * * * *

Naomi does a series of front walkovers, down a mat.

"Nice work, Naomi. But point your toes in the air!" Dominique calls out.

On a second row of mats, Abby and Kim do double cartwheels. The girls laugh as they rotate.

"Your hair is tickling my leg," Abby giggles.

"Hey, you just kicked my head," Kim counters.

"I didn't mean to."

"No talking while tumbling," Dominique says.

"Sorry," the girls say as they continue cart-wheeling down the mat.

Avelyn preps for a back walkover.

"Try lifting your leg to start," Dominique suggests.

"How do you mean?" Kelsi asks.

Dominique walks over and motions for Kelsi to lift her leg. Kelsi raises her right leg up. Dominique raises it to a perpendicular level.

"Start here."

Kelsi nods. She raises her arms above her head, bends back and kicks over.

"Good. Now try lifting it higher."

Kelsi smiles and preps again. She lifts her leg to about 120 degrees, then does another back walkover. Dominique nods approvingly.

Avelyn waits at the end of the mat.

"Go ahead."

Avelyn bounces up and down, then steps back and points a toe. She runs in three big strides and lunges into a round-off, then back handspring. She rebounds beautifully and springs straight up.

"Excellent. Wanna try a tuck?" Dominique asks.

Avelyn excitedly shakes her head. Sabine opens the door and enters the room. There's a flurry of tumbling and tricks around the room. She looks at it all, unsure.

"Come, come, and join in," Dominique says.

Sabine half-smiles and leans against a ballet barre. Dominique walks over to her.

"Oh, come on. Get in the action."

"That's really alright. I'll just watch for a minute and see what's going on."

"Nonsense," Dominique declares. "Kick up to a handstand."

"What?" Sabine asks, surprised.

"Kick up to a handstand. Don't worry; I'll hold your legs."

Sabine scrunches up her face as if ready to cry.

"Come now, we haven't all day."

Sabine kneels down and puts her hands on the floor. She lifts one leg up. Dominique stares down and smirks.

"Alright, whatever works."

She grabs Sabine's leg and yanks her up. Sabine squeals.

"Ah, don't worry; it won't hurt....too much."

Dominique holds both Sabine's legs. Sabine scampers to keep her hands on the ground.

"Push!"

Dominique tightly holds her legs. Sabine tries to kick them apart. Dominique holds them tighter against her chest.

"First lesson. Legs together."

Sabine whimpers as she holds the handstand position.

* * * * * * * * * * * * * * * * * *

Shawna and Denver fold up a mat and drag it to the corner of the room. Miss Donna walks in, as Dominique talks to the girls.

"And I want all of you to work with rubber bands to further your stretch so we can hold those fun positions I taught you earlier. Also, do the barre work daily. It's the skeleton of your technique."

"So, how's the choreography coming?" Miss Donna asks as she walks further into the room.

"Choreography? We didn't do any choreography today. I have to get to know the skills of my performers first. Then I'll set the piece based on their skills."

Miss Donna nods. "Alright then." She looks around, uncertain what to say in response to Dominique's methods. She spots pictures of herself on the wall and smiles. "Well, did everyone have a good time, then?" she says ever so chipper.

"Yeah."

"Yes."

"Uh, huh."

"Totally."

The girls all shake their heads excitedly. Sabine just smiles a blank smile.

I have a headache.

Miss Donna nods, "Good."

"You have an excellent group of hard workers here," Dominique comments.

"I like to hear that. And hard workers, just so you know, tomorrow, the seamstress will be here to take measurements, so I suggest you manage your portions tonight. Salad perhaps," Miss Donna says.

A couple girls groan.

"Remember, it's not what's on the outside that counts, it's what's inside. But that doesn't mean your outside can't look good. And muffin tops are not attractive," Miss Donna looks at Kim.

Kim frowns.

I got my period. I'm just bloated. She thinks to herself.

"Well, see you all tomorrow. Come ready to work."

CHAPTER 6: MEASURING UP

"Miss Donna agreed with us," Mrs. Howser says as she wraps her arms around Sabine. "Ooo, honey. What is that?" She touches Sabine's stomach and feels a small pooch. "You have measurements today, what did you eat?"

Sabine shrugs, "It's just a little water weight. It'll be gone by lunch time."

"I hope so. You don't want your costumes to be too loose because you're measuring big today of all days."

"Mother, it really isn't that big of a deal."

"Yes it is. We have everything set up. This is your year. How many times do I have to keep telling you that?"

Obviously again.

* * * * * * * * * * * * * * * * * * *

The seamstress, Regina, measures Kelsi's waist.

"24 inches. Perfect ballet body proportions. You should be a ballerina," she says.

"Funny you should say that, I just..."

"I need to be measured now. I have a manicure in ten minutes," Hilary interrupts.

"I'm almost done. I'll be with you in a minute," Regina says.

"Maybe you didn't hear me. My cuticles are popping out. This is a beauty emergency!"

Miss Donna steps out in the hallway. Regina writes down Kelsi's measurement.

"Is there a problem?" She asks.

Regina shakes her head, "Nothing here."

"I have to go right now but she won't let me," Hilary complains. "My manicure is in…" She looks at her cell phone. "Eight minutes."

"It will only take a few minutes, I'm sure." Miss Donna says.

"I was just going to call my dad. Anything you want me to tell him?" Hilary waves her cell phone in the air.

Miss Donna's eyes widen.

"Regina, can you please stop with Kelsi and take Hilary first?"

Regina looks at her questionably. "Whatever you say." She sighs.

Hilary quickly steps in front of Kelsi.

"And take one inch off each thigh plus my waist. I'm getting a seaweed body wrap this week. I'll lose at least an inch for sure," Hilary says confidently.

Kelsi steps back and watches Regina measure Hilary.

What just happened? Who died and made her Queen of the Universe?

* * * * * * * * * * * * * * * * * *

"Is anyone going to see Hilary today?" Miss Donna asks.

"I am." Bailey raises her hand in the air. "I'm going to her house after she gets back from her beauty treatments."

"Can you give this to her?" Miss Donna says as she hands her a piece of paper. "And here's yours as well."

Bailey looks at the sheets of paper.

"$3000?" she gasps. "But that's almost twice as much as last year."

"We have to step up our game, costumes included. This year we're going for Broadway caliber," Miss Donna says. "Kelsi." She hands Kelsi a sheet of paper.

Kelsi looks at the paper. "$3000, my mom is not going to be happy."

"Know what you mean," Bailey mutters.

"I'm dead meat. That's only for five numbers. Gosh that works out to what…"

"Six hundred per costume."

"That's insane."

"Maybe we could all have a garage sale or something and raise money to pay for everything," Bailey suggests.

"Good idea," Kelsi half-smiles. "That could be a lot of fun."

"Look at my nails, chickies," Hilary busts through the doors. She struts right over to Bailey. "Like?"

Hilary's fingernails are painted gold with intricate black designs on each nail. She wears a pink Guess warm-up suit and black and pink high-tops.

"Yeah, they're beautiful. They must have cost a fortune."

"Nothing daddy's credit card can't handle," Hilary replies.

Kelsi walks away with her sheet of paper. She looks down at the $3000 in bold lettering followed by the due date.

That's only two weeks away. Oh man, this is going to be a long night.

* * * * * * * * * * * * * * * * * * *

Sabine sits in the passenger seat, her mother drives.

"And the first three competitions are all the small local ones so we can dominate those easily."

"Dominate. You'll destroy," Mrs. Howser says.

"Then we have Co Dance in Chicago, followed by the Pulse in St. Louis, and finally Tremaine in Detroit."

"Perfect." Mrs. Howser grins widely.

* * * * * * * * * * * * * * * * * * *

"And Nationals are in New York, Orlando and Hawaii. It's gonna be so much fun!" Hilary giggles.

"That's a lot of traveling," Bailey says.

"Oh, it will be fun. My dad will let us use his private jet to get there."

"All of us? Like the whole team, that's awesome."

"Well, not everyone. But don't worry you made the cut."

Bailey looks unsure at her. Hilary grabs her hands and holds them.

"Stick with me and I'll take care of everything."

* * * * * * * * * * * * * * * * * * *

"Darling, I know you're excited, but..."

"Mom, did you see the schedule? We're hitting all the biggies this year. It's going to be amazing. We'll be competing with the best girls in the nation and learning from the most famous teachers ever," Kelsi explains.

"I know, and that's all great and all but these fees," Amanda Little points to the paper in her hand. "$3000 for costumes? What happened to the twenty dollar leotards we used to buy when you were small? You girls looked adorable."

"We don't want to look adorable. We want want to look incredible," Kelsi explains. "We want to look like showgirls."

"I thought you were going ballet bunhead on me. No make-up, no fancy hair. What happened to that girl?"

"And I thought you wanted the make-up and glitter."

"Not at a $3000 price tag."

"But mom…"

"Kels, it's not just the costumes; it's the travel fees and competition costs and we already spent $5000 on your summer intensive. I don't know how we're going to manage all this," Amanda explains. "I mean, I really wish you had been accepted at New York. Tuition there would have been less expensive than all this combined."

Kelsi lowers her head. *I'm a failure.*

"I don't know what we are going to do," Amanda says, "but we'll make it work somehow. I have to talk with your father."

Kelsi nods and then looks down again.

If I had only gotten into NYCB. Things would be different. Things would be fine. I have to show them they didn't waste their money on me. I have to win.

CHAPTER 7: SOLOS

"And pretend to shoot the arrow," Dominique yells. Cecilia pretends to shoot an arrow and the target is a stacked pyramid with Hilary at the top. She falls and is caught by Harmony and Naomi. Under her, Avelyn jumps down doing a huge Russian split. She tumbles forward with a back-handspring, into a back tuck.

The rest of the pyramid spreads out doing a series of animalistic, tribal funk moves. Sabine is in the back. She completes all the dance moves and grimaces as she preps for partner cartwheels.

"And rest," Dominique yells.

Everyone stops and breathes heavily.

"It's coming along. How do you all like it?"

"It's awesome," Shawna says.

"I love the funkiness," Abby adds.

"Plus the music is super cool," Molly says. Denver nods in agreement.

"Good, now I'm going to teach you a new trick. It's a combination of a scorpion and a flying leap," Dominique says.

Sabine raises her hand.

"Yes, go ahead, Sabine."

Sabine runs out of the room.

"Man, that girl has to pee a lot," Dominique mutters under her breath. A couple girls hear and giggle.

* * * * * * * * * * * * * * * * *

Mr. Fred watches the tap routine and nods happily.

Sabine is in the front. Bailey is behind her. The two fight for his attention.

Stamp stamp brush toe heel dig heel toe heel heel smack

Sabine smiles at Mr. Fred.

Watch this wing. And that one. Oh, and here's a little shuffling off to Buffalo for ya.

Bailey smiles at Mr. Fred.

Kelsi and Avelyn smile as they look at the two competing. Hilary bangs a couple sticks together in the back and taps her toe. She is not a happy camper.

This is so gay. This is so gay. This is so gay.

She continues to smack her sticks together, a look of displeasure painted across her face.

* * * * * * * * * * * * * * * * * *

Denver and Kim shake their heads around, their hair flies around crazily. Wild 80s music plays. They shimmy and shake. Naomi and Harmony spin into the center of the room and prep for a series of fouetté turns.

Standing on the side of the room, Bailey leans into Hilary and whispers, "Solos are posted today. Can't wait to see if I got one. I hope I did. I've tried really hard this year."

Hilary bites her lip. "Yeah, I mean if I don't get one I'll like go crazy on Miss Donna 'cuz I deserve one more than anyone."

Bailey looks at her seriously. Hilary corrects herself, "You too. You and I deserve one."

Hilary bites her lip again. She then jetés into the center of the room behind Bailey and joins in on warp speed ponies.

What if I'm not picked? What will I do? My dad better have taken care of this for me!

* * * * * * * * * * * * * * * * * *

"Mothers and daughters. Think a mother passing her little daughter off," Miss Donna says as Harmony and Molly cradle Cecilia and Abby then pass them to Denver and Shawna.

Kelsi, Avelyn, and Sabine walk into the center of the room and slowly extend their left legs into the air. Their legs all reach 180 degrees. The girls hold the position for a moment then, grab their legs and complete a double-leg turn. They finish turned out in an arabesque on eleven.

"Beautiful!" Miss Donna exclaims. She touches her eyes,"Ah, so touching."

She claps.

* * * * * * * * * * * * * * * * * *

Stephanie, the receptionist, a blonde college-aged girl, posts a paper on the hallway wall. The girls all wait anxiously.

"Have at it," She says and walks away.

The girls rush over. Harmony pushes to the front. Her finger trails down the page. The paper reads:

This year's competitive solos

- Avelyn

- Sabine

- Kelsi

And a duet, by Hilary and Bailey

"Ah, shucks," Harmony says as she sees the list.

"I got one!" Avelyn screams.

She jumps up and down, as Bailey quickly scans down the list. Hilary grabs her shoulders and spins her around.

"You're with me!" Hilary yells.

"What?"

"We're together. We're doing a duet."

"A duet?"

"Isn't that great. Best friends forever."

Hilary raises her fist and the girls hit fists then bump hips and finally blow a kiss at one another.

"Miss Donna's never done a duet before." Bailey says.

"Guess she just knows what good buds we are and how we do

everything at like the exactly same time 'cuz we're so much alike. And like, she wanted us to be perfect and not compete against each other."

Bailey just nods, "Yeah. Sure."

Kelsi watches the two and giggles.

Glad it's not me.

She looks at the list.

Kelsi. That's me. I got a solo!

Avelyn's at her side with her and in the air. They high five each other.

"Please be musical theater," Sabine crosses her fingers and closes her eyes.

"Oh, my gosh. That's me. That's my name." Sabine says.

She jumps into a huddle with Avelyn and Kelsi. The three giggle and laugh.

Everyone else disperses.

"Poor Bailey." Avelyn says.

"What?" Sabine asks.

"She got stuck with Hilary," Kelsi says.

"Aren't they like Siamese twins or something though?" Sabine jokes.

"Practically," Avelyn says.

"Just glad it's her, not me," Kelsi states.

"Amen to that," Sabine adds.

All three laugh.

"Three weeks 'til competition," Kelsi says.

"Let's all kick butt," Sabine says.

They put their hands together and raise them up at the same time. "Kick butt."

I hope I win. Avelyn thinks as she looks at Kelsi smiling.

Mom will be happy. Now the real work begins. Beating Kelsi and Av. Sabine contemplates as she jumps up and down excitedly.

This should be fun. Miss Donna will probably give me jazz. I kinda wish it was a ballet solo, though. Kelsi thinks as she imagines pretty pink pointe shoes on her feet.

* * * * * * * * * * * * * * * * * * *

The song "Mama Who Bore Me" plays. Sabine does an arabesque into an inside pirouette, then stops facing the mirror and is that what you wanted? should it be develops or the way you spelled it? her right leg to the side. She smiles.

* * * * * * * * * * * * * * * * * * * *

Kelsi dances to a Lady Gaga remix. She jives and jumps and spins and kicks. She moves a million miles a second and maintains complete control. Kelsi finishes with a turned in triple pirouette and jumps to the floor in middle splits, then looks up.

"Fierce," Miss Donna says.

* * * * * * * * * * * * * * * * * * * *

"It's from that cool show 'Wicked'. I play a witch and lip sync this really neat song with lots of emotion and tempo changes," Avelyn tells several of the girls.

"Sounds great. Can't wait to see it," Kelsi says.

"It's really fun. I can't wait to see yours either. And yours, Sabine. I heard it's heartbreaking."

"I don't know about heartbreaking. But it is quite emotional," Sabine says.

"Anyone know about Bailey's duet?" Kelsi asks.

"You mean Hilary's solo," Cecilia says.

"What?" Kelsi says surprised. "Did Bailey quit?"

"No, nothing like that. It just might as well be Hilary's solo the way she talks about it."

"So, what is it?"

"Don't know. They won't say. Every time someone asks they just say you'll have to wait and see. Then, when Bay's not around, Hilary goes on and on about how great she is and how she stands out. It's sickening," Cecilia continues.

"Tell me about it," Sabine adds. "She makes me want to puke."

"Maybe I'll ask her," Kelsi says.

Just then, Bailey walks in with a slick side ponytail held by a glittery clip at the nape of her neck. She touches the clip to check that it is still in place.

Kelsi waves, "Hey."

Bailey shyly waves back.

"So, how's your duet coming?" Kelsi asks.

"Good. It's fun."

"That's good," Kelsi bites her lip, nervous. "What are you guys doing? What song?"

"Well, it's a--"

Hilary walks in. Identical hairdo down to the sparkly clip. "It's none of your business," She completes Bailey's sentence as she walks to Baliley and adjusts her hair slightly.

"I think Bailey can speak for herself," Kelsi says.

"That's what she was going to say. Wasn't it, Bailey?"

Bailey looks between Kelsi and Hilary, confused.

"It's none of her business, is it? She's just jealous, huh?" Hilary prods.

Bailey weakly nods and lowers her head.

Kelsi rolls her eyes.

Avelyn scowls, "You're such a brat, Hilary. No one likes you."

Hilary sticks out her tongue.

"Oooo, so scary. No one likes me boo hoo," she says sarcastically. "Bailey likes me. And you all better be scared cause we're gonna take this competition down. It's called being a winner. Either you're a winner or you're a loser."

Several of the girls stare at Hilary and scowl.

"I think you all know what you are," she smirks, then tosses her pony over her shoulder.

Avelyn lunges at her. Sabine holds her back.

"Let me go. I'm gonna pull those fake extensions out," Avelyn says.

"Not worth it. Be smart," Sabine reasons with her. "She's not worth it."

Avelyn relaxes. Sabine releases her arms.

"Who does she think she is?" Avelyn asks aloud.

"God," Kelsi jokes.

The tension melts away and the girls chuckle.

"Come on; let's go dance our butts off," Kelsi says. The girls all file into one of the dance rooms.

* * * * * * * * * * * * * * * * * * *

The girls do chaîné jetés across the floor. Bailey goes and has great extension of her legs on her jetés. Avelyn is next in line. Hilary pushes her out of the way.

"Let me show you how it's done," she blurts.

Hilary does her chaîné jetés. They're mediocre at best; she doesn't get very high and her feet are flexed.

Avelyn stares at her from across the room and misses her cue to go.

"Go!" Miss Donna yells.

Avelyn snaps out of her daze as Hilary smiles an evil little smile at her. Avelyn chaînés to a deep plie then springs into the air. She travels extremely high and her flexible back arches as she rolls to the floor and immediately turns into the next set.

"Lovely," Miss Donna says.

Avelyn reaches the end and brushes past Hilary, bumping her.

"Oh sorry, I didn't see you there. Must have been too low to see," She remarks.

Hilary just scowls and folds her arms across her chest.

Miss Donna notices and sighs.

* * * * * * * * * * * * * * * * * * *

"Av, time for dinner!" Mrs. Behm calls.

Avelyn, fully dressed with a coat, boots and scarf, runs down the stairs.

"Mom, it's the annual bowling night," Avelyn says.

"I still don't understand why you girls stay out late bowling the night before a competition."

"It's just for the first competition, which we dominate any way."

"True. But still. It's a matter of principle. You're growing girls, you need your sleep."

"Yeah, yeah."

Mrs. Behm raises her eyebrows.

"Love you, mommy." Avelyn kisses her mom on each cheek and heads for the door.

"Uh, excuse me?" Mrs. Behm says.

"Oh, Denver's mom is picking me up. That's alright, isn't it?"

"Denver's mom…."

"The nurse. The one who never comes to competitions," Avelyn explains.

"Ah, that's right. No wonder I can't remember her."

Avelyn smiles.

"Be safe."

"Always am."

Avelyn rushes out the door.

* * * * * * * * * * * * * * * * * *

The bowling alley is packed with junior high and high school kids. Music plays and light flash around.

"Look at him, he's cute," Molly says as she points at a teenage boy flexing his muscles for some other girls.

"Too short," Sabine says.

"I like his shirt though," Kim adds.

"Not bad. Go talk to him," Shawna says.

"Talk to a boy. No way," Molly replies. "I just like to look."

A couple girls giggle.

"I wonder what it's like to kiss a boy," Kim mentions.

"You've never?" Cecilia asks.

Kim shakes her head, "You have?"

"Only the posters on my wall." She laughs. "You guys haven't kissed a boy, either?"

The girls look at one another, most shake their heads, "no." A couple girls remain silent.

"Never mind. New subject. Who has homework?"

"I hate homework," Molly says.

"I know; I was just trying to change the subject."

"From what?" Hilary asks. She emerges from the restroom area.

"Boys," Harmony chirps.

"Now that's something I'm an expert on."

"Really?" Kim says.

"I'm Hilary. Hilary. Everyone knows how many boyfriends I've had."

Kim just stares at her. "So how many?"

Hilary suddenly freezes.

Ummmm.....

"Hey, look at Abby." She points at Abby who spins around in circles with her bowling ball.

Miss Donna approaches and catches the ball, stopping Abby's rotation. She removes Abby's fingers from the ball's holes.

"No broken fingers."

Abby smiles and nods, dizzily. She steps to the side and falls over into a chair.

"What am I doing?" Miss Donna mumbles to herself.

She motions for the girls all to gather around.

"I just want to thank everyone for coming to our annual bowling party. This night is supposed to be fun and give each of you a chance to mingle with your dance friends outside of the studio. So play, bond, and eat up. I brought lots of healthy snacks." She motions to an untouched vegetable and fruit tray. "Just no competition tonight. Play for fun."

Miss Donna walks over to a group of parents standing by.

"Bet you can't get a spare, even with the bumpers," Hilary says to Avelyn.

"Bet you I can get a strike," She retorts.

"Bet you can't get two."

"Make it a turkey."

"Bet you're a turkey," Hilary replies.

"How much you want to bet?"

"A hundred bucks."

"How about twenty?" Avelyn asks.

"Deal." She looks at Kelsi. "Double the odds?" she asks Avelyn.

"You and Bailey, versus me and Kelsi."

"Double my investment. I like it," Hilary says.

"You're on."

Avelyn walks back to Kelsi. "You feel lucky?"

"No. And I don't have twenty bucks, Av."

"You don't need it. We're gonna win," Avelyn says.

"Hope so."

"Trust me. Pretty girl doesn't want to mess up her fake nails. Just watch."

Kelsi looks at Hilary who files her nails and then carefully inserts her fingers in a bowling ball.

Kelsi steps up to the line and preps. She brings her ball back, then forward, and releases it. The ball doesn't travel very fast, but it's straight. The ball hits the head pin. All the pins around fall down. Kelsi jumps up.

"Yay! I did it!"

Hilary flips her hair over her shoulder. "This is competition."

Bring it on, Hilary. Bring it. Avelyn thinks as she stares at the massive preparation Hilary puts herself through, in an attempt to get her nails in the ball without being scratched.

Hilary preps herself. She moves her feet around like Fred Flintstone and approaches the lane on tip-toe. She swings her arm back and the ball drops behind her.

"Ah, my nail!" she screams.

The girls all giggle, except Bailey who rushes to her side. Miss Donna is quick to follow.

After a moment, Hilary walks back to the scoring table. Bailey wraps a bandage around the tip of Hilary's finger.

"Smooth move, Hil." Avelyn says. "Hope your duet is that great tomorrow."

Hilary rolls her eyes and huffs.

I'll show you. My hip hop is gonna rock.

CHAPTER 8: FIRST COMPETITION

"Competition day. Competition day. Competition day, hey, hey!" Bailey sings. Hilary laughs at her as they sit in the back seat of the car.

"We're gonna kill 'em with our duet," Hilary says.

"I just hope we do well. I love getting up there and dancing."

"Do well? We're gonna win. I can't wait to see the looks on their faces when they see us up there with the trophy."

"The look on whose faces?"

"Oh, no one," Hilary says with an evil smile on her face.

* * * * * * * * * * * * * * * * * *

The girls are gathered in a large ballroom converted into a dressing room. They're all dressed in animal skin pattern costumes with ragged edges and asymmetrical necklines.

Miss Donna walks in. "Everyone ready?"

The girls smile and nod, as they stretch in their own little groups; Hilary and Bailey together; Avelyn, Sabine, Kelsi and Cecilia in another clump; Molly, Shawna, Kim and Abby and the rest together in their own circle. Miss Donna notices the separation.

"Let me get everyone together," she says.

The girls all huddle close together and encircle Miss Donna. Some are excited and bounce around. Sabine is nervous and takes deep breaths.

Just get through acro and it will be fine.

"I first want to say that I am really proud of the work you have done so far this year, each and every one of you!" She looks around at the girls and they all sigh or give sappy smiles.

"And I know that everyone might not always get along all the time, but we're a family. We're a team and we have to work together. You have to work together. I wish I could be out there with you getting everyone happy and excited, but I can't. You have to find that inside yourselves."

Kelsi looks across the circle at Hilary and Bailey who hang on one another.

I hope she's happy.

Kelsi sighs.

"Even if you don't like someone for whatever reason, you're in this as a team. So put aside the competitiveness. Put aside the anger, the frustration, the whatever. Just go out there and dance, because that's something you all have in common; you love to dance."

A couple of girls understandably nod.

"You do love to dance, right?"

Several girls nod. A couple say, "Yeah."

"What was that?"

"Yeah," More girls say.

"I'm sorry, I can't hear you," Miss Donna continues.

"Yes!" The girls all scream.

Miss Donna smiles.

"Good. Now give me some sugar."

She reaches out her arm and puts her hand in the center of the circle. Her fingers flutter. The rest of the girls join in so all their hands meet.

"Let's..." Miss Donna begins.

"Rock it!" The girls scream.

Miss Donna smiles.

Rock it! Gotta love being a Rockette. She smiles to herself at her own play on words.

She proudly struts out of the dressing room.

"Animal Instincts, you're up." A woman pokes her head into the room.

Molly jumps up. "Guys, that's us. Let's go."

The girls rush out of the dressing room.

* * * * * * * * * * * * * * * * * *

On stage, Avelyn does a round-off back-handspring into a back tuck, toward the judges. She spins around and drops to a middle split. All the others tumble in from the sides with cartwheels and walkovers. They all drop to one knee and hit a pose.

The audience claps. Miss Donna hoots and hollers.

* * * * * * * * * * * * * * * * *

Toe tap, toe tap, wing, wing, delayed wing. The girls shine on stage, despite their rather ordinary street attire. The girls form a line and turn around. All of a sudden, the girls rip off their street clothes to reveal sparkly flapper style one-piece outfits.

Abby smiles. *Gosh, I love sequins.*

* * * * * * * * * * * * * * * * *

Shawna enters with a huge battement.

Denver next.

Kelsi smiles as she pirouettes into a back attitude turn.

Kim joins in with a kick, and the group continues with a kick line.

Hilary does a body roll that begins a round of rolls as the dancers travel seamlessly to a new formation.

They all join together for the chorus. Kick hold step dig head shoulder hip, hip.

The girls shine on stage as they perform "Cell Block Tango" with a cellblock stage prop in which they dance in and out of.

* * * * * * * * * * * * * * * * *

Next up is lyrical. In nude-colored, backless dresses the girls take the stage. The fronts of the dresses are covered in nude-colored rhinestones which shine under the bright stage lights. The song is moving. The judges watch Avelyn's incredible extensions with tears in their eyes. Bailey rocks Hilary in her arms like a baby as the song ends. The audience goes wild. The judges are all smiles as they write on their score cards and talk into their individual microphones.

* * * * * * * * * * * * * * * * * *

"Just jazz left," Harmony comments to Naomi as they change into white dresses with neon-colored dangling circles sewn across the bottoms. Each girl has her own crazy hairstyle from crimpled extensions to afros, to bejeweled masses of tangled hair. The girls head out of the dressing room together.

* * * * * * * * * * * * * * * * * *

All the dancers at the competition sit on the stage. Each studio forms its own little group. The girls and guys chatter as the MC looks over his list.

"And the top ten junior large group dances are…"

All the dancers on stage suddenly turn their attention to him.

"Number ten, You Can't Stop the Beat."

A small girl jumps up, as her teammates all clap and yell. She runs to the front of the stage and takes a trophy from the MC.

"Number nine, and top tap routine for the competition. Tap This."

Sabine's eyes widen.

"That's us!"

"Go, go!" Kim yells.

Sabine jumps up and accepts the trophy from the MC, then goes to the back of the stage and collects a handful of medallions. She passes one to each girl on the team, as the MC continues the countdown.

"Number six. Cell Block Tango."

"Woot, woot!" Hilary yells. "Sexy little beotches are we!"

She hops up and walks to the front, her hips sway with each step. She takes the trophy and struts back, stopping to look at her make-up in the trophy's reflection.

"And now, the top five."

A drum roll is heard.

"Number five. The fiercest number I've seen in a long time. Please welcome to the stage, Animal Instincts."

"I got this one," Avelyn says. She runs to the front of the stage. The MC holds the trophy and smiles with her for a picture from the photographer, in front of the stage.

"Now young lady, tell me where you learned those crazy animal moves."

"From Miss Dominique Rene," Avelyn says.

"Wow. Impressive."

Avelyn nods.

"And the name of the studio?"

"LBT Dance Company," Avelyn says proudly.

"Thank you very much, sweetheart. And congratulations to you and your animal friends."

* * * * * * * * * * * * * * * * * *

"I can't believe 'Mothers and Daughters' got first," Denver says as she hugs a humungous trophy.

"I know and jazz got second. We kicked butt!" Abby says. The two slap hands.

"Too bad we didn't sweep it though," Hilary says. "At my old studio we always swept the top ten."

"We didn't even have ten routines. We only had five," Sabine reasons.

"I know. I'm not dumb."

"No comment," Sabine says and walks away. "I have to get ready for my solo."

Bailey walks up to Hilary.

"What's wrong?" She asks as Hilary scowls.

A vibration is heard. Hilary pulls her phone out of a pocket in her jacket. She looks at the screen and giggles.

"What is it?" Bailey asks.

Hilary just looks at the screen and giggles again as she texts.

"What's so funny?"

Hilary looks at her then turns her attention back to the phone screen. She chuckles once more.

"Can I see?" Bailey moves into Hilary to look over her shoulder and see the phone.

Hilary steps away and covers the phone.

"Personal space, Bay. Learn it, live it, love it."

Hilary walks off and continues to text. Bailey sadly watches her. She looks up at the clock.

"We have our duet," She calls after Hilary.

Hilary raises a hand and motions her away.

Bailey taps her foot nervously and bites at her cuticles.

Who is she talking to? We only have ten minutes. I thought she'd want to practice it again.

Kelsi sees the diss from afar but is busy with her headphones on running through her solo. Avelyn notices as well, but she too is busy getting dressed.

* * * * * * * * * * * * * * * * * * *

"They're next, hurry," Naomi says to Kim. The two run hand-in-hand to the audience and sit with the other girls.

Kelsi, Avelyn and Sabine all sit together.

"Time to see what the secret has been about," Avelyn says.

Bailey and Hilary walk out on stage and strike their poses. Bailey is crouched down on the ground and Hilary stands with her arms folded across her chest, head down.

The music starts; it's a hip hop remix of "Me and My Shadow."

"I love this song," Denver says.

Me too, Kelsi thinks.

A kick cross step, get low, get low. The girls work it out, grooving and locking to the beat. Hilary is cocky but it works on stage. Bailey is cool and confident. She glides smoothly from one groove to the next. At the end, the routine shifts into a crazy fast beat and the girls do a krump-style combo in perfect unison. It's exciting and heart pumping. The girls rise to their feet and clap along.

"Move it!" Denver calls.

"Work it out!" Molly chimes in.

"Go, go, go, go!" Cecilia says as she pumps her fist in the air.

Bailey and Hilary hit their final poses. The audience enthusiastically claps.

"That was actually really good," Sabine says.

"Yeah, it was," Kelsi agrees.

"Bailey knows her hip hop," Avelyn comments.

Hilary and Bailey run off stage.

Hilary rushes ahead.

"That felt awesome," Bailey says bursting with energy.

No response.

Hilary just continues to walk ahead of her.

"Hey, wait up."

Bailey rushes to catch up. She gets to Hilary's side and sees she's texting on her cell phone.

"Hey, good job out there. I think we did really well. Don't you think?"

"Uh, huh," Hilary says without even looking at her.

"Who've you been texting all day?" Bailey asks.

"A friend."

"Oh cool. Someone I know?"

"From school."

"Oh, okay."

Bailey continues to linger at Hilary's side.

"Wanna go see the solos?"

Hilary texts and laughs.

"Well?"

Hilary turns and looks at her as if just noticing she was there.

"Hmm?"

"Wanna go see the solos with me? We better hurry to make sure we get a seat."

"No thanks."

Hilary walks off and continues to text. Bailey, saddened once again, watches her walk off

What's her deal today?

* * * * * * * * * * * * * * * * * * *

The music plays. A heavy synthesizer starts a pattern that will stick in your head.

Kelsi, in a simple leotard and matching skirt with rhinestone detailing, dances on stage.

Pas de bourrée, step, prep.

Why does this feel so much like ballet?

Kelsi completes a triple pirouette. She pumps her arms straight into the air and shakes her shoulders back, then begins a complicated sequence of arm movements with alternating feet. Then she leaps into a stag, where she kicks herself in the head.

"Hitch layout and down. Chase switch and reverse stag, break.

She lights up the stage with personality and movement. You could actually see her dancing behind Lady Gaga doing this routine. No space goes untouched. She falls flat on her back to finish.

The audience claps.

"Good job, Kels!" Amanda yells from the front row.

She breathes heavily. Her chest contracts deep in and then pushes back out.

"That was really good," Sabine says from the wings of the stage.

"Really good," Avelyn repeats standing beside Sabine.

Is she going to beat me again?

* * * * * * * * * * * * * * * * * * *

"And the champion solo goes to Kelsi Little for 'Lady Gaga Craze'." The MC says.

Kelsi stands and steps through people to make her way to the front of the stage. The MC hands her the big trophy. They pose for a photo and then he asks, "That was incredible. Where did you get all that stamina from?"

"A lot of ballet classes," Kelsi jokes.

The MC looks confused. He shakes his head and continues, "And tell me the name of the studio again."

"LBT Dance Company," Kelsi says. She smiles. Her mom blows her kisses. Kelsi curtsies with her trophy.

* * * * * * * * * * * * * * * * * * *

"What does your Tuesday night look like?" Mrs. Howser asks Miss Donna. "I'd really like to get Sabine in for at least three privates with you before the next competition. And I think we should do some major re-choreographing if she's going to stand any chance of winning, don't you think?"

"Every competition is different. It's all subjective. And you have to admit, she really wasn't the best today. It was someone else's trophy this time. But if you want I can pencil you for a few days."

"Oh, thank you, thank you so much."

"I don't know how much we can do as far as changes…"

"Just make it sparkle. Harder than ever before. She can handle it. I'll make sure of it."

Miss Donna slowly nods, "Alright."

"Oh, and her costume," Mrs. Howser begins. "It really needs some work. I'm not happy with it. She needs something better. Bigger, brighter, more...more..."

"Broadway?"

"Exactly!"

"I'll see what I can do."

Mrs. Howser grabs Miss Donna's hands.

"Thank you. This means more to me; I mean Sabine...more than you know."

"No problem. My pleasure," Miss Donna says, grinning through her teeth and thanking her stars that most moms are not this invested in their kids dance routines.

Miss Donna walks away, as Sabine approaches her mom.

"Things okay?" she asks.

"More than okay. Miss Donna has agreed to do some privates with you before Co Dance and she's certain you'll win there. So, don't worry about today. Co Dance is important. This, this is just a stupid little amateur hour. At Co Dance you'll dominate."

Mrs. Howser wraps her arm around Sabine's shoulder.

"Trust me; I'll make sure of it," She finishes.

Sabine looks up at her mom, curious.

What is mom up to now?

Mrs. Howser rubs Sabine's head and hugs her as she thinks about a slightly unethical plan.

We got this one in the bag.

CHAPTER 9: DANCE, SLEEP, REPEAT

"Again. Kelsi beat me, again," Avelyn says. Her frown pulls down her beautiful eyes and cheekbones.

"You did great, honey. I'm proud of you," Mrs. Behm says. She leans against the wall beside the front door to the studio.

"It was alright. I messed up my back jeté into the body slide across the floor."

"You're the only one who noticed."

"And Miss Donna."

"Did she say anything to you?" Mrs. Behm asks.

Avelyn thinks hard. Her eyes search the sky for an answer.

"No."

"You were the only person who noticed."

"You're just saying that 'cause you're my mom and you're supposed to," Avelyn says.

"No. I could tell you that you were a horrible mess with horrible technique and atrocious stage presence but you weren't. That would be a lie and..."

"Lies are a sin," Avelyn finishes.

Avelyn uncrosses her arms and paces.

"It's just...I always lose to her. I'm tired of it." Her eyes fill with tears.

"Sweetie, Kelsi did a really good job and so did you. It just so happens that at this competition the judges liked her dance a tad bit more. At the next competition, they might like your dance more and then she'll come in second," Mrs. Behm tries to reason.

Avelyn avoids eye contact and swipes away the tears.

"Besides, she's your best friend. Aren't you at least happy for her?"

Avelyn nods.

But I want to win.

"Well, she'll be happy for you, too, when you win."

When exactly will that be?

Avelyn looks up and fakely smiles at her mom as her eyes fill again.

"Thanks mom. You're the best."

She hugs her.

"Ah, I love these. Glad you're not getting too old to hug your mom."

"Nah. Maybe in college. But you still got me for a couple more years," Avelyn jokes.

"Good. Now go on in there and congratulate your friend again," Mrs. Behm says.

Avelyn nods and picks up her dance bag. Mrs. Behm waves and walks off to her car. Avelyn watches her in a daze.

I wish Kelsi had stayed in New York. I know that's terrible, but then I'd be the winner. I'd be the star. Wonder if she'll go back. She does like ballet…weirdo.

* * * * * * * * * * * * * * * * * * *

"Hey, Sab!" Kelsi says surprised as she enters the main dance room. Kelsi has been doing her barre in the waiting room, as she has done every day before class. She didn't realize anyone was in the studio.

Sabine spins around, startled. She is covered in sweat and breathes heavily, "We could have warmed up together."

Avelyn, Naomi and Denver enter.

"Why are you so sweaty?" Naomi asks.

Sabine just wipes her brow and takes a deep breath. The rest of the girls enter and toss their bags on the side, then spread out to talk and stretch.

"Practicing hard before class?" Kelsi asks.

Sabine half nods but doesn't really acknowledge her. She looks around as she nods and continues to catch her breath.

"Why is she so tired looking? Class hasn't even started." Avelyn says to Kelsi.

Kelsi shrugs, "Don't know."

"Huh."

Avelyn tosses her bag on the side and fixes her shoes. Kelsi watches Sabine walk to the side and grab a couple tissues. She wipes down her face, arms and neck.

Miss Donna must have worked her hard.

Sabine takes another deep breath and looks in the mirror.

This better work.

She wipes another bead of sweat from her hairline.

Hilary enters and steps to the side. She texts on her cell phone. Bailey enters the room a moment later. She looks at Hilary and then sets her bag down several feet away.

"Great job on the hip hop routine," Avelyn says to Bailey.

"Thanks."

"Yeah. It was pretty killer," Molly adds.

"I knew you had it in you," Kelsi winks.

Hilary quickly comes to Bailey's side.

"Thanks. I...I mean, we, were really happy with it. I think we'll win every competition, don't you think?" She says.

"Maybe," Avelyn says. "The bigger ones are harder to place at."

"Just have to wait and see," Kelsi continues.

"Yeah, well..." Hilary purses her lips and stares them down.

Avelyn and Kelsi look at Bailey.

"Good job, again."

"Yeah, good job," Avelyn says.

Bailey smiles and stands upright. "Thanks."

They turn and walk to the other side of the room.

Hilary stares Bailey in the eyes as Bailey looks off across the room at Avelyn and Kelsi.

"They're just saying that to make you feel better because you didn't get a solo this year," Hilary says.

Bailey's smile fades.

"They didn't really mean it," Hilary continues.

You didn't get a solo either.

Bailey looks back longingly at Avelyn and Kelsi who smile and laugh.

CHAPTER 10: TROPHY LIFE

Kelsi's legs shake nervously as she sits in the passenger's seat of her mom's car.

"Excited for competition? You didn't seem this excited the last two," Amanda Little says.

"I am. But really I just can't stop thinking about next week. The convention," Kelsi says.

"Co Dance?"

Kelsi nods.

"The first biggie of the season."

"Yep." Kelsi looks out the window.

And my first chance of the season for a scholarship. And Co Dance has ballet!

"What?" Amanda asks.

Kelsi's nose scrunches up.

I didn't say that out loud, did I?

"I didn't say anything," Kelsi replies.

"Huh. Must be hearing things."

Kelsi nods. "Maybe it was the music." She turns the volume knob louder on the stereo. The music begins to blare. She rocks out to the music. Amanda frowns and turns it back down.

"Some of us are older, you know, and don't like music blaring."

"Older? You mean ancient," Kelsi jokes.

Amanda gasps.

"Just kidding, mom. Gotta keep you on your toes."

"Trust me, you do."

They both smile and stare ahead.

A scholarship from Co Dance…now that would be awesome.

* * * * * * * * * * * * * * * * * *

"Sydney just twisted her ankle," Cecilia calls.

The girls in the dressing room all scamper around getting into their acro costumes and practicing tricks.

"What are you talking about?" Kim asks.

"She was just going up the stairs and rolled it," Cecilia explains.

"Another reason to take the elevator," Kim shakes her head.

Miss Donna enters the dressing room. Sydney follows closely behind hobbling.

"Alright girls we only have a couple minutes. Syd here is still in the routine but we need to make a few changes and tweak things a bit."

The girls quickly gather around.

"Go to the first set of lifts."

The girls form two separate circles.

"Okay, Sabine, I'm going to need you to step into her place."

"Me?" Sabine asks quietly.

"You were the understudy, right?"

Sabine shyly nods.

"Well, then…"

Sabine steps into Syd's place. Sydney moves into the back.

"You know what to do, right?" Miss Donna asks.

Sabine nods, "Yes."

No.

"Take me to the ending pose then. Dominique said this would need some improvement."

The girls run into their places for the ending pose.

"Okay, so Sabine you'll have to do the walkovers into that spot."

Walkovers?

Sabine's eyes widen.

"You can do walkovers, can't you?" Miss Donna asks.

"Well…" Sabine starts.

"They're not that hard."

Miss Donna stares Sabine down. "Just go out there and do it." She claps and motions for the girls to rush out of the dressing room.

Oh shoot, oh shoot.

Sabine swallows hard as she rushes out with the others.

* * * * * * * * * * * * * * * * * * *

During the lift sequence, Sabine stumbles and almost drops Denver's leg. Naomi's eyes nearly pop out of their sockets as she stares across and is left holding Denver's entire weight by one leg alone.

Then, during the final tumbling pass into the final pose, Sabine falls out of her first front walkover and misses the second one. She poses on her knee, trying to get up off the ground in time for her standing pose. Holds for ten. Bows.

The girls walk off stage.

Harmony scoffs at Sabine. Denver elbows her.

"What was that all about? I almost fell on my face. "

"I'm sorry. I just slipped," Sabine defends. "I caught you eventually."

* * * * * * * * * * * * * * * * * * *

"I can't believe acro didn't even place," Molly says as she looks in the bathroom mirror at the medallions around her neck.

"It's all Sabine's fault," Abby growls. "She screwed it all up."

Abby grabs a paper towel to dry her hands.

"Maybe Miss Donna will kick her out of the dance," Molly says.

"Hopefully," Abby says as she and Molly leave the restroom.

Sabine steps out from a bathroom stall. She stares at the door.

"I'm sorry," she says weakly. Her eyes well with tears.

Kelsi steps out of another stall.

"Oh, no," she walks to Sabine and hugs her. "It's alright. It happens."

"But they're right. It really was my fault. I shouldn't be in the number."

"Since when did you start listening to anything Molly or Abby has to say? Come on, they're silly," Kelsi reassures.

"But..." Kelsi covers Sabine's mouth.

"But, nothing. Get ready for your solo. You're a showstopper."

Kelsi smiles and washes her hands, then gets two paper towels. She hands one to Sabine to dry her hands with.

"Thanks."

"Hey, that's what friends are for."

"We're friends?" Sabine asks.

"Why wouldn't we be?"

Kelsi leaves the restroom. Sabine looks at herself in the mirror. She stares hard; unsure of whom she is looking at.

* * * * * * * * * * * * * * * * * *

Avelyn and Kelsi each pose for a picture with two large trophies. The camera flash goes off. Avelyn looks at her trophy and hugs it.

"Good job," Kelsi says.

"Thanks. You, too."

Kelsi lifts up her big trophy and walks away. Mrs. Behm approaches Avelyn.

"I'm so proud of you," she says with a hug.

"Mommm," Avelyn says, slightly embarrassed.

"See, I told you that you could do it."

"But we tied for first. I didn't win," Avelyn says.

"A tie is a win in my book."

Avelyn rolls her eyes.

"Either way, I'm really proud of you," Mrs. Behm says with a smile.

"Good performance, Av," Sabine says.

"Thanks. You too."

"Yeah, you really deserved that style award."

"Thanks. See you later."

Sabine waves and walks off with Cecilia's family.

"Where's Mrs. Howser?" Mrs. Behm asks. "I tried to find her when I was looking for a seat before solos, but I didn't see her."

Avelyn thinks for a moment.

"I don't know. Actually..."

Denver walks by.

"Denver," Avelyn calls.

Denver stops and raises an eyebrow.

"Have you seen Sabine's mom?"

Denver bites her lip as she thinks. She scrunches her nose and shakes her head.

"Weird, huh?" Avelyn says.

"Yeah," Denver says and then continues to walk away.

"She's always at competition. She'd never miss Sabine dance. Hope she's okay," Avelyn says as she looks up at her mom, worried.

"Maybe something just came up," Mrs. Behm tries to reassure.

Avelyn nods, unconvinced.

That really is strange...

CHAPTER 11: FATIGUE, FEARS & FRIENDS

"I'm home!" Mrs. Howser calls as she enters the house. Sabine rushes out of her bedroom. "So?" Mrs. Howser questions, eyebrows raised.

"Fourth overall and a best style award."

Mrs. Howser sets her bags down quietly. "Oh."

Sabine's face drops. "Oh?"

"Oh, I mean good job. But fourth? That means you wouldn't even stand on the podium at the Olympics."

"Olympics? What are you talking about?"

"Sabine...this is very serious." She places her hands on her daughter's shoulders. "I just spent the weekend registered as a teacher for the Co Dance convention in Tulsa."

"Are you allowed to do that?" Sabine asks.

"Don't worry about it." Mrs. Howser flips her hair back. "As a teacher I'm allowed to see the routines ahead of time. And I videotaped them."

"Cool."

"Not cool. Very cool."

"Yeah, that's what I said."

"No, you're not getting it." She takes a moment to stare at Sabine. "That means I have all the routines you're supposed to learn next week for the convention. You know the one where you compete for scholarships?"

Sabine's eyes widen. "So, I can..."

Mrs. Howser nods.

"And then I'll..."

Mrs. Howser nods again.

"Oh my gosh. How awesome. Thank you, mom."

She throws her arms around her mother's neck and hugs her tightly.

"Now, I expect you to practice every day. That way you'll be ready and stand out." Mrs. Howser says.

"This is so cool. I can't wait to tell the girls and show them."

"No!" Mrs. Howser yells.

Sabine backs up.

Mrs. Howser gulps, "I'm sorry. I meant no, you cannot do that, sweetheart. You don't want your friends to be jealous of your mom and how smart she is. Instead, let's just keep this our little secret. Okay?"

Sabine slowly nods, "Kay."

"Good girl." Mrs. Howser kisses her head. "Now go on and practice." She hands her the video camera.

Sabine takes it into the living room and connects it with a cable to the television. Footage of the Co Dance instructors going through the routines with their assistants pops up.

This is so cool. I'm gonna win a scholarship for sure.

Sabine starts to follow along with the dance movements.

* * * * * * * * * * * * * * * * * *

"So, the plan is everyone's going up on Friday and we'll have our traditional pool party swim late at night, then eat ice cream sundaes when Miss Donna isn't around, and basically have a big slumber party in someone's room, Kelsi says.

Amanda tosses a salad and scoops it into bowls.

"I'm sorry, honey, but two nights at the Chicago Marriott costs an arm and a leg. Your dad and I just don't have that kind of extra cash lying around."

"I know, but…"

"Honey, couldn't we just go up Saturday and meet the girls there?" Mr. Little says as he enters the kitchen and gives his wife a kiss on the neck.

"Ewe. PG," Kelsi says as she covers her eyes.

"A kiss? Come on, Kels," Mr. Little says.

"Gross. Parental contact is not for children's' eyes."

Amanda giggles. "Someday you'll like a boy and want to kiss him and I'm going to do the same thing to you."

"And if you do kiss him I'm gonna kick his butt." Mr. Little says.

"Stop," Amanda jokes. "There will come a day."

"Well…" Kelsi starts. They both turn and look at her, scared. "Topic change…I could just go with Avelyn and stay with her family. She said it would be okay."

Mr. and Mrs. Little breathe a sigh of relief.

"Gosh, I thought you were going to say you already had a boyfriend." Mr. Little says.

"Well…" Kelsi teases.

Mr. Little flashes his eyes at her.

"Well, what do you think of that idea?"

"Honey, it's a fine idea but I really don't want to do that to Mrs. Behm. She's already helped out so much with taking you to class and things through the years."

"She really doesn't mind," Kelsi continues to try.

"Not this time," Amanda says as she places the salad bowls on the table. "We'll all just drive down early Saturday morning so you'll be ready for the classes and come home each night. Sorry."

"No. I understand. You guys sacrifice a lot so I can dance," Kelsi says sadly.

What I need is a job. A job and a scholarship!

* * * * * * * * * * * * * * * * * *

"Congratulations to you!!!" Avelyn's family sings. Her mom, dad and little brother all clap as Avelyn blows out the candle on her ice cream cake.

"Thanks guys."

"Hurry and cut it. The ice cream's gonna melt if you start blabbering," her little brother complains.

Avelyn takes the knife to cut the ice cream cake and looks at it unsure where to start.

"Here, let me at it," Her father says.

"Good job, sweetie," Mrs. Behm says.

"It was just another dance thingy. Big deal," her brother moans.

"You like the cake, don't you?" Avelyn asks.

Her brother stuffs his mouth with cake. He thinks for a second, then nods.

"That's what I thought." She smiles.

"And next time you'll get first all on your own," her brother blurts as her parents try to shush him.

I hope so. I don't know, though.

* * * * * * * * * * * * * * * * * * *

Avelyn tosses and turns in bed. She looks at the clock; it reads "1:00 a.m."

Can I win next week? Do I have homework?

She turns on her computer and looks at Facebook for a while. She sees pictures from last weekend and today on the studio's page.

Kelsi is better than me. Everyone likes her better. The judges like her better.

Avelyn looks at the website for the New York Company Ballet.

Does it make me a bad friend that I wanted her to stay? She's a ballerina now. I know it. She doesn't want to be here. Maybe I can convince her to go back. Then I'll be the best. Then I'll win first every time.

Avelyn looks at the clock; it reads "2:00 a.m." She turns off her computer and tries to fall back asleep.

If I do a triple instead of a double there, and then hold that extension for an extra beat, will that change things?

Avelyn continues to toss and turn.

If she fell like Sydney, she wouldn't be able to do her solo.

She suddenly sits up.

"What am I saying? She's my best friend."

I'm sick. I really am. I need to see a doctor. I wouldn't think things like that. I'm nice.

She lies back down.

Right?

The clock reads "4:00" when she finally falls asleep. At "6:00" her alarm goes off. She jumps up and is startled.

"Kelsi!"

Avelyn looks around and realizes where she is, then takes a couple calming breaths.

"I need to get some sleep." She looks at the clock. "Oh, school, how I hate you."

She plops back down on her back.

* * * * * * * * * * * * * * * * * * *

Miss Donna plays the music for the jazz dance. The girls rehearse in the large dance room of the studio.

Cecilia and Harmony sparkle, with their big smiles, as they spin onto stage to complete a double pirouette followed by splits on the floor and then rise up over their toes with a body roll. Molly, Shawna, Kim and Abby move forward with a running arm pattern and head-shaking sequence. Bailey and Hilary enter from one side with a tombe pas de bourrée second jump. Kelsi crosses downstage of them, from the other side. Kelsi looks in the mirror and realizes Avelyn isn't behind her. Confused, she turns her head to the side and sees Avelyn staring off in a daze.

The music stops.

"Avelyn!" Miss Donna yells.

Avelyn hops. Her arms fly down to her side and she instantly spots Kelsi on the opposite side of the room.

Shoot.

"What are you doing?" Miss Donna yells.

Avelyn doesn't know what to say?

Trying to sleep?

"Well?"

"I...I...just missed it," she mutters.

"You missed your cue, that's what you did! Unacceptable. Now everyone has to start from the beginning, just for you. They're all tired and ready to leave, but you're making them do it again."

I'm tired, too. Trust me. Try doing this on two hours sleep.

"You should be ashamed of yourself," Miss Donna says coldly.

Avelyn cowers.

"From the top, ladies. Thank Avelyn for that one," Miss Donna scowls.

Avelyn looks down. Kelsi returns to her side. She looks at her, then turns away.

Wonder what's going on. Avelyn never misses a cue. She counts music better than anyone.

* * * * * * * * * * * * * * * * * *

Avelyn downs a Red Bull before heading into the dance studio. No missing cues this time.

* * * * * * * * * * * * * * * * * * *

Avelyn tosses and turns in bed.

I have to win. I have to win. I have to sleep. Breathe in…breathe out…

The clock reads "3:00 a.m."

This sucks. Babies can sleep. My brother can sleep. My parents are asleep. What's wrong with me?! Ok. Ok. Relax all my muscles. Why won't my brain just turn off?

* * * * * * * * * * * * * * * * * * *

Avelyn stands at the counter of a coffee shop.

"Cappuccino, please."

"Shot of espresso?" the man behind the counter asks.

"Double, please."

The man looks at her questionably. Avelyn smiles. The man turns around to make the drink. Avelyn's smile fades. The bags beneath her eyes sag further.

* * * * * * * * * * * * * * * * * * *

In class, Avelyn starts to nod off. A girl beside her, Courtney, taps her desk as the teacher turns around to face the class. Avelyn sits up quickly.

"Avelyn, do you know the answer?" he asks.

"Uh…" She looks down at her notes. "Yes, it's 65."

"Excellent," the teacher turns back to the white board.

Avelyn looks at Courtney and mouths, "thank you." She then reaches in her backpack and pops open a Red Bull. Avelyn quickly takes a sip, then sets it back in her bag.

* * * * * * * * * * * * * * * * * * *

Several of the girls wait in the hotel lobby with their parents and armfuls of luggage, rolling costume racks and large make-up cases.

"So, what time for the swim tonight?" Denver asks.

70

The girls all turn away and moan.

"How 'bout ten?" she says.

No one answers.

"Guys, it's a tradition," she continues. "Then we have to pick a room for the ice cream slumber party. I'd say we could use mine, but my brothers snore and it's kinda gross."

"I'm not really feelin' it this year, Denver," Shawna says.

"What?" Denver questions.

"Yeah, I'm kinda tired. Abby says. Kim nods in agreement.

"But...but it's a tradition."

"Traditions die," Hilary says. "Everything dies. Get over it. Ice cream parties are so last year!"

Hilary brushes past and whips her hair in Denver's face. Denver sighs, as the girls all begin to disperse in different directions with their families and luggage.

"But we always do it," she says weakly. "We're a team."

* * * * * * * * * * * * * * * * * *

Avelyn plops down on the bed and quickly falls asleep. Her mom looks at her and smiles. She pulls a blanket up and tucks her in, then sweetly kisses her forehead.

* * * * * * * * * * * * * * * * * *

In the room next door, Mrs. Howser and Sabine sit on the bed together and watch the dance videos on their video camera.

"Don't forget that look," Mrs. Howser says. "That's something everyone will forget because they footwork is so fast. You'll get their attention with that in a second."

Sabine studies carefully.

* * * * * * * * * * * * * * * * * *

Bailey and Hilary jump around on the bed. Hilary stops, but Bailey continues. She giggles and hits Hilary with a pillow.

"Stop," Hilary says.

Bailey freezes. "What?"

"I'm done, alright."

"But we were just--"

"Gosh, Bailey sometimes you're so immature," Hilary groans.

Bailey sits down on the bed.

"Well, what do you want to do?" she asks.

"Watch Real World on MTV."

Hilary grabs the remote control and changes stations.

"But I'm not allowed to watch that. My mom says it's too crazy or something. A bad influence."

"You're such a baby, Bailey. Your name should be baby. Maybe I'll start calling you that."

Bailey scowls.

"Hey, that's not nice."

"Hey, that's not nice." Hilary mocks. She finds MTV. "Here we go."

"I told you I can't watch this."

"You're lame. My other friends and I watch this all the time. I should text Michelle right now actually."

Hilary grabs her cell phone and begins texting. She giggles.

Bailey looks sideways so she won't see the television. She spots a phone book and picks it up and flips through it. Hilary sees what she's doing and shakes her head.

"Your mom's not even here, how would she even know?"

Bailey turns to face Hilary.

That's a good point. She wouldn't know. It's not like she'd ask me if I watched MTV anyway.

"Come on," Hilary pleads. "Be a friend. Watch it with me."

One time won't hurt, Bailey thinks.

She turns and leans back against her pillow. She and Hilary begin to watch the program together.

CHAPTER 12: CO DANCE

"Classes all morning, then competition starts at two," Kelsi explains as her mom pulls into the parking lot.

"So you need me back when?" Amanda asks.

"My solo goes on around 3 o'clock."

"Alright. Dad and I will back then with bells and whistles on."

Kelsi raises her eyebrows. "Mom."

"Oh, just get in there and get yourself a scholarship."

"That's not 'til tomorrow."

"Oh, that's right."

Kelsi shakes her head.

Silly mom! How many years have I done this? Like since I was a mini?

"See you later, kiddo," Mr. Little says.

"Bye dad. Bye mom." Kelsi runs into the building.

* * * * * * * * * * * * * * * * * *

A group of girls and guys bust out moves on the dance floor. A hundred or so other dancers stand on either side and watch. Several mark the moves.

"Next group!" an assistant yells.

The girls and guys switch, and another thirty people spread out on the makeshift dance floor.

Sabine hits every move perfectly, but she lacks the hip hop style and bounce. Hilary and Bailey stand out. Hilary shows off a total attitude which makes her look stuck-up, but her rhythm and swagger are sensational. Bailey just makes hip hop look easy.

* * * * * * * * * * * * * * * * * *

Hilary bounces around as she shows off a ribbon which says "excellence". She floats the ribbon over Bailey's face and chants, "I got one. You didn't. Nah nah nah nah nah."

Avelyn and Naomi stand with their arms crossed and watch.

"What happened to sweet old Bailey?" Naomi asks.

"Oh she's still sweet. She's just BFFs with the devil," Avelyn says. Naomi chuckles.

"What? It's true," Avelyn continues.

Naomi nods,"Yes."

* * * * * * * * * * * * * * * * * *

"Watch your turnout," Judy Rice, the ballet instructor who makes everyone like ballet class, says as a group does a ballet combination of petite jetés and coupes. Kelsi glances down at her own turn out, her knees and hips are completely flat, perfect turn out. She focuses strongly in front of her.

Arms. Arms. Don't show tension in your arms.

Kelsi's arms suddenly lighten a bit and flutter. Judy instantly notices and watches her for a moment. She whispers in her assistant's ear and the assistant nods.

Sabine notices and dances harder. She has all the steps, whereas some other dancers miss things and keep going. But her technique just isn't there. She relaxes her feet at times, and her legs aren't turned out properly from the hips. Still she pushes on, and tries to impress the teachers.

* * * * * * * * * * * * * * * * * *

Avelyn and Bailey hold up their ribbons.

"Contemporary queens," Avelyn says.

Kelsi gallops over with a ribbon in her hand.

"And our ballet princess," Avelyn says.

All three girls giggle.

"Hopefully, this means we'll be in the running tomorrow," Kelsi says.

"Scholarships?" Bailey asks.

Kelsi nods.

"Would be nice," Bailey says.

"Really nice," Avelyn elaborates.

They all hug in a huddle.

Bailey looks at Avelyn and Kelsi, and smiles.

The three amigos.

"So, you sure you don't want to spend the night with us?" Avelyn asks Kelsi.

"Nah, mom doesn't think it's a good idea this time."

"Why?"

"She says it's an inconvenience."

"Inconvenience? You're like family," Avelyn says.

Kelsi shrugs, "Moms rules. No biggie."

Sabine walks up to them. She is exhausted from dancing so hard. She looks at their ribbons, jealous.

"You kicked butt on that contemporary, Sabine. I thought you were gonna get a ribbon for sure," Bailey says.

Me too, Sabine thinks.

"Yeah, ya know," she says.

"You did do really well. Like the best I've ever seen. You picked it up so quickly. I'm jealous," Kelsi says.

"Not quick enough I guess," she points at their ribbons.

"I bet you'll get one tomorrow. Or a scholarship even," Avelyn says.

"Hopefully," Sabine says. "I'm gonna go get ready for solos."

"Kay. Bye." Kelsi says.

Sabine takes off.

"Poor thing. She tried so hard," Kelsi sympathetically frowns.

"She's a big girl. She can handle herself," Hilary interrupts. "Bailey, you ready?"

Bailey looks at Avelyn and Kelsi, searching for a reason to stay.

"I was gonna go get an ice cream with the girls actually," she says.

"We have a duet in an hour and a half, and you're thinking about ice cream? God, what a selfish partner I have," Hilary moans.

"Sorry. You're right." She drops her head and starts to walk away with Hilary then turns back. "See you later."

Kelsi and Avelyn watch her walk away.

"Tragic."

"Train wreck."
They both shake their heads.

* * * * * * * * * * * * * * * * * *

Sabine is on stage dancing her solo. Her costume has more rhinestones and accessories than before. She reaches further, extends her legs more and her toes are perfectly flexed and arched over in point at different moments.

Dressed in their own solo costumes, Kelsi and Avelyn watch from the audience. Their faces are full of awe.

Sabine does a perfect illusion. She turns and does left fouetté turns, followed by right fouetté turns.

Kelsi leans into Avelyn, "Did you even know she could do that?"

Avelyn shakes her head.

Sabine reaches up toward the sky and then pulls into her heart. She slowly and smoothly slides to the floor. The girls are in complete shock and awe. They are frozen and clap slowly as everyone around them claps loudly with aggression.

"Was she holding back?" Kelsi asks.

"Guess so."

"There were definitely some changes in that."

"Yeah. You could say that."

"She might win."

"I think she will."

"Good luck."

"Yeah, you too."

The girls continue to stare in shock at the stage.

* * * * * * * * * * * * * * * * * *

"First place goes to 'This Woman's Work'!" Nancy O'Meara, the MC for this portion screams.

"Told you," Avelyn says.

"At least we tied for second," Kelsi says.

"Yeah, second's good."

Not.

"Second's great," Kelsi says.

Sabine jumps up and poses with her trophy. She kisses it for a picture.

* * * * * * * * * * * * * * * * *

Mrs. Behm shakes Avelyn.
"Darling, time to get up."
Avelyn blinks, groans and rolls over.
"Avelyn, you have a big day ahead of you."
"I don't want to go to school," Avelyn moans.
"No school today. Dance!"
"Too tired."
"Av, you have lyrical first with Nick. Then ballet. It's scholarship day! Your favorite," Mrs. Behm tries to entice her.
"Later," Avelyn pulls the covers over her head.

* * * * * * * * * * * * * * * * *

Molly pushes Shawna's leg down as she lies on her back with her leg pulled into her chest.
"Scholarship day. I hope I get it," She says.
"Harder," Shawna says.
Molly pushes down harder on Shawna's leg.
"Good?"
"Harder."
Molly suddenly pushes all her weight into Shawna's leg. Shawna squeals in pain and rolls over on her side.
"Aghhhh."
"Oh my gosh. Are you okay? You said harder. I am soo sorry!"
Shawna holds her leg in pain and crouches into a ball.
Avelyn holds a Red Bull in one hand and a cup of coffee in the other. She sips from both.
"Need a kick today?" Abby asks.
"What? Huh?" Avelyn says, jittery.

* * * * * * * * * * * * * * * * *

The girls struggle with a ballet combination in the center. Avelyn shakes as she tries to balance in passé. Kelsi moves through positions with ease and shows off long neck and ballet body. She shines.

I'm in heaven.

She smiles inside and out, as she dances.

* * * * * * * * * * * * * * * * * *

Avelyn and Bailey spin on their knees and hop up onto their feet.

Shake, shake, shake and slide.

Avelyn uses all her extra energy to power through the tiring number.

Pump, contract. Pump, contract.

Bailey ignores Hilary beside her. She just dances for herself and has fun.

The teacher, Barry Youngblood, points to Bailey and Avelyn.

"Dance with the final group."

Bailey jumps up, excited. Hilary shakes her head, dissed. She makes a face at Bailey.

"What?" Bailey says.

Hilary stomps off, anger written all across her face.

Bailey and Avelyn dance with the final group and repeat the hip hop routine. The girls watch on the side.

"Go, Bailey! Go, Av!" Kelsi roots them on quietly from the side.

Bailey continues to dance with enthusiasm. Avelyn jumps with energy. All of a sudden Avelyn blanks. She stops and stares off in a daze.

I...I...

Kelsi watches wondering what's going on.

Did she blank? No get back in there, Av. Do it.

Avelyn looks around, and then runs in tears, off the dance floor.

* * * * * * * * * * * * * * * * * *

Tyce stands in front of the group of guys and girls.

"We're gonna do a number straight from that little show you might have seen, 'So You Think You Can Dance.'"

The dancers cheer loudly.

"Oh, so you've seen the show," Tyce jokes.

"Yeah!" Several dancers scream.

"Well let's get to it. It's harder than it looks," Tyce says.

He plays the music. It's from Sweet Charity.

The dancers all scream again.

Tyce begins to teach the dance. Sabine seems to know it, but so do several other dancers, so no one really notices.

Hilary tries hard, but she can't manage to master the moves. Tyce points out Kelsi, Avelyn, Sabine and Bailey, as well as about ten dancers from other studios. Hilary doesn't make the cut.

During the final grouping, Tyce notices Avelyn's extra energy.

"Nice," He says.

Avelyn smiles widely, even though she feels like she might pass out.

Kelsi pats her back and grabs her, as she almost trips over her own feet as she walks to the back of the room.

* * * * * * * * * * * * * * * * * *

"And now the scholarships," Nancy announces.

The girls and guys all excitedly gather around.

"Here we go, here we go!" Kelsi bounces around.

Sabine presses her lips together tightly and smiles.

Time to win!

"We have five scholarships today," Nancy continues. "All the dancers with ribbons got our attention, but these are our top picks of the weekend. So, come on up when we call you, and get your award and a picture with the faculty. In Tap, please welcome up, Sabine Behm."

Sabine slowly walks up to the front and takes her paper. She poses for a picture with Gregg Russell.

"For Contemporary, please welcome up, Georgina Kinder."

A short girl rushes up and hugs Gina Starbuck, then takes a photo with her.

"In ballet..."

Kelsi crosses her fingers.

"Kelsi Little."

Kelsi looks down at her fingers. She looks at Avelyn and Cecilia, unsure she heard her name. They both nod.

Kelsi goes up to Judy Rice, takes the photo and receives a paper. She excitedly rushes back to her friends.

I did it!

"In one of my favorites, Hip Hop by Barry Youngblood, please welcome up, Bailey Saunders."

Bailey freezes.

"Did Nancy just call my name?" she asks.

Kelsi nods and hugs her.

"Ahhhhh!" she screams.

Bailey runs up and practically jumps at Barry. He laughs, and they take a photo.

"And last, but not least, as this one was a really hard decision," Tyce starts.

"It's Avelyn for jazz. It has to be," Kelsi says to Sabine.

"For jazz, please welcome up, Kingston Leighton."

A thin teen boy runs up and hugs Tyce. Disappointed, Avelyn looks at him. Surprised, Kelsi and Sabine look at one another.

Avelyn frowns, then yawns.

"I need to go to bed," She says and starts to walk away.

I tried so hard. I don't understand.

CHAPTER 13: WARDROBE MALFUNCTION

Avelyn shakes her head, as she drinks yet another Red Bull. She pastes a number across her chest. Naomi puts another sheet of paper with the same number on Avelyn's back. *Another convention. Another chance for a scholarship. Red Bull save me.*

Avelyn looks tired. Her eyes have dark bags under them and her smile is less enthusiastic and less genuine than normal. Avelyn fights to keep her eyes completely open.

Hilary arrives in a tiny black bikini top and briefs. Her hair is slicked back with sparkly gel, and she has lots of make-up highlighting her eyes and lips. Everyone stares at her as she walks in.

Yeah, I know I'm hot stuff.

She struts even more confidently.

Bailey enters several feet behind her, trying to avoid association. She shakes her head as Hilary walks.

Miss Donna turns and sees Hilary.

"Morning, Miss Donna," Hilary smiles. She drops her dance bag, pulls out a mirror, and puts on more lip gloss.

Miss Donna examines her, appalled by what she sees.

"Hilary, I think you should put on a sweatshirt. It's a bit cold in here, and I don't want you getting sick?" she says kindly.

"I'm fine, thanks."

"Hilary, I really think you should put on a shirt at least."

"I have one. See." She points to her barely there bikini. "And look, it jiggles." She turns around and shows off the beading on her boy cut bikini bottoms which jiggle up and down when she shakes her butt.

"Oh my!" A mother passing by says. Embarrassed, Miss Donna lowers her head.

"Hilary, I need you put some dance clothes on right now, or I cannot allow you to dance today."

Hillary sighs, "Fine." She reaches into her dance bag and pulls out a crop top. She pulls it over her bikini; it doesn't even cover her belly button.

Miss Donna shakes her head again. "At least it's something." She looks around at all the girls. "Good luck ladies, make me proud." She walks out of the room.

Hilary sticks her tongue out at Miss Donna, as she walks away. The moment the door closes behind Miss Donna, Hilary pulls off her crop top and tosses it on her bag.

I'm gonna get noticed. No one's stopping me.

Bailey rolls her eyes, as she watches Hilary continue to shake her butt, and point to the scandalous beading, as she snaps pictures of herself on her iPhone.

* * * * * * * * * * * * * * * * * * *

The combos begin. Kelsi and Cecilia dance beside one another as they learn the choreography. They see Sabine in the row ahead of them.

"She's really been on lately," Cecilia says.

"I know," Kelsi replies.

Strange huh. Perfect timing for it though.

Avelyn, tired, goes the wrong way on a step and bumps into Harmony.

"Ouch," Harmony says. "You stepped on my foot."

"No, I didn't. You're in my way." Avelyn says.

Harmony glares at Avelyn for a moment then returns her focus to the teacher.

Avelyn marks the steps, while everyone else does them full out. She elbows another girl.

"Watch it," the girl says.

"What?"

"You just hit me."

"No, you hit me. It's your fault," Avelyn argues.

"What?"

"If you have been staying in your own spot it wouldn't have happened."

The girl looks at Avelyn like she's crazy.

Hilary and Bailey dance beside each other. Hilary does all she can to make her beads jiggle and show off her body by sexing up each move. Dressed in booty shorts and a long sleeved Lululemon shirt, Bailey tries to distance herself and moves over a person in line, while Hilary is busy grinding the air during a second position plie jump.

Kelsi watches the assistant, Mia Michaels, do a sauté step kick step prep, pique turn into an arabesque hold. Sabine does the step prep and pique turn at the same time as the assistant on stage.

How did she know that was coming?

The group does the short combo full out. Sabine only marks it.

Why isn't she practicing?

Kelsi completes the combination and takes a breath as the Mia talks. "Okay, take it from the top. Remember the breath and the look," she says.

They run through the dance, up until that point. Sabine half-marks the routine, doing the footwork, but no turns, leaps or extensions.

Is she saving her energy or something?

"One more time, then we'll break you into groups," Mia says.

Kelsi pushes harder this run-through. Mia sees her in the back row and nods. Sabine once again half-marks the combo. Kelsi is confused.

* * * * * * * * * * * * * * * * * *

Cris Judd claps his hands, "Let's break up into groups and see what we've got."

His assistant walks around the group of dancers and divides them into sections. Bailey steps to one side, so she is in a separate group from Hilary. The first group spreads out. Hilary pushes her way to the front row.

The dance begins. It's a quirky little number full of directional changes, torso moves, arm sequences, and body rolls. Hilary holds totally still and shakes her butt during the freestyle. Cris notices and looks the other way. "That's just wrong," he mumbles to his assistant.

The dance ends. "Next group," he says. Hilary walks toward him.

"I just wanted to tell you I love your work."

"Thanks."

He says. "Put on a shirt next time. That top should really only be worn at the beach."

"Oh, no, you gave us a good workout. I'm all hot and sweaty," she wipes her forehead.

"Next group," Cris calls and walks away.

Hilary smiles and bounces to the side.

He noticed me! It worked.

Cris just shakes his head.

That's the wrong kind of attention. That girl has trouble written all over her. And she's like twelve?!

Hilary continues to smile, as the next group dances.

Any attention is good attention. At least I'm known. Someday I'll be famous.

The other girls just completely avoid her.

Bailey is in the last group. She dances in the front row and doesn't miss a beat. Sabine is beside her and hits the moves like she has been rehearsing this for months. The two are pure fun to watch, the joy that exudes from them is contagious. Cris pulls both girls aside at the end of the routine.

"Wanna join me on the stage?" he asks.

Sabine nods her head quickly up and down, "Yeah. I mean yes!"

Bailey nods and runs up the stairs and joins the assistants on stage. Cris follows. He talks into the microphone.

"Okay, we only have time to do it two more times, so let's make these incredible."

The music starts. Bailey rocks it out on stage. Sabine looks almost as good as Cris's assistant. She doesn't normally rock hip hop like this. Kelsi watches her on stage, as she dances on the floor at the same time.

So weird. She is almost like, TOO good.

* * * * * * * * * * * * * * * * * *

"But it will get them to look at us even more," Hilary says.

"Like they won't be already?" Bailey says.

"You have to be realistic."

"Realistic? It's a duet! Of course they'll be looking at us."

"I don't see what the problem is."

"That's not our costume."

Hilary points to her bikini top. "This is a lot more flattering than that silly pants thing they put us in."

"No, it's not."

The other girls watch as the two fight in the corner of the lobby area at the hotel.

"Someone should go over there," Kim says.

"And say what?" Denver asks. "You're a freak, Hil, no one likes you."

"Yeah, that'd go over real well," Abby laughs.

"I feel bad for Bailey," Molly says.

"Soooo glad I didn't get the duet," Shawna says.

"You weren't even in the running," Molly jabs.

Shawna's jaw drops. Molly's eyes widen. She covers her mouth.

"I mean…I mean…" Molly starts.

Shawna runs up the stairs.

"Shawna wait! I didn't mean that!" Molly calls as she runs after her.

"Drama, drama, drama," Cecilia adds.

"Tell me about it," Kelsi says.

She and Avelyn continue to watch Bailey and Hilary go at it. Sabine and her mom start to walk down the stairs and stop at the landing.

"I'm not wearing a bikini top for hip hop. My mom would kill me," Bailey says adamantly.

"Why can't you just go with the flow? I know what's best," Hilary tries to convince her.

"No, my mom knows what's best."

"Like not watching MTV," Hilary smirks. "I could tell her about how much you love the Real World."

"That show was stupid."

"Doesn't matter, you watched it, didn't you?"

"Only because you made me."

"Did I hold your eyes open and make you?" Hilary crosses her arms and stares at Bailey.

"No," Bailey barely spits out.

"Wear the bikini top, or I'll tell your mom everything."

Bailey looks at her. Her eyes almost water with tears. She bites at her bottom lip. She looks over and sees Kelsi and Avelyn in the middle of the lobby.

"No."

"I am so telling your mom."

"Go ahead. She won't believe you anyway," Bailey walks toward the bathroom.

"Fine. Be that way," Hilary growls. She stomps off.

Avelyn sighs, "I'm gonna go. See you tonight?"

"With bells and whistles on," Kelsi says.

Avelyn heads down stairs. She slows her steps as she overhears Mrs. Howser's voice farther down the stairwell.

"Well?"

"The dances are easy when you have a week to practice," Sabine says.

Avelyn's eyes widen. She stops on the stair and leans into the stairwell to listen.

"You'll be a shoe in for a scholarship," Mrs. Howser says.

"I better. I've been working hard. I know those dances better than anyone else."

"We'll just have to wait and see," Mrs. Howser says, delighted.

"I'm kinda hungry," Sabine says.

"There's a salad bar down the street. Let's go there."

Mrs. Howser and Sabine start to head up the stairs. Avelyn slips behind a door. She waits until they pass. Mrs. Howser looks around, thinking she heard something.

"Come on, mom. We don't have much time," Sabine says.

Mrs. Howser continues up the stairs.

Avelyn opens the door and takes a deep breath.

"That was close."

* * * * * * * * * * * * * * * * * * *

Avelyn sits on her bed and thinks. A puzzled look comes across her face.

The dances are easy when you have a week to practice. What does that mean?

Her mom sits down on the bed beside her.

"Everything okay?"

"Yeah." Avelyn says, startled. "I was thinking I might take a nap."

"Good idea."

Mrs. Behm tucks her into bed. "I'll leave so I won't disturb you."

"You never disturb me, mom."

Mrs. Behm kisses her forehead and leaves the room.

You're a shoe in for a scholarship...I should be, I know the dances better than anyone else.....

Avelyn sighs.

So weird.

CHAPTER 14: WEAK PULSE

Several of the girls stretch backstage. Avelyn and Kelsi stretch out their middle splits on the ground, beside each other. Kelsi looks around, and spots Sabine talking with her mom on the side.

"Have you noticed how good Sabine has been at learning the dances?" Kelsi asks.

"Yeah," Avelyn nods.

"The last couple weeks. It's like...it's like she knows them."

"I know. She looks really good in all the classes."

"Really good."

Avelyn stares at Sabine hard.

She knows them. She has to.

"I wonder if there are any rules against learning the dances ahead of time?" Avelyn questions.

"How would you do that?"

"I don't know. Who knows the dances they're gonna teach?"

"The assistants," Kelsi says.

"So you'd have to be an assistant to see them then?"

"I guess. Or if you were at another convention."

Avelyn continues to stare at Sabine.

She's getting them ahead, somehow. So not cool.

* * * * * * * * * * * * * * * * *

Miss Donna stands with Kelsi, Sabine and Avelyn, all dressed in their solo costumes.

"You did great, girls. But I don't want you to get your hopes up for placing in the overalls. The competition here is really fierce and you just never know. I saw a girl out there that looked like she was twenty competing in your thirteen year old category. Who knows what's going on?"

"I'm happy either way," Kelsi says.

"Me too," Avelyn agrees.

"I'm thrilled. I just can't wait 'til scholarship announcements," Sabine says.

"Now, we do need some cleaning up. Things have been getting a big messy lately."

The girls all look worried.

"But we'll take care of that next week."

Bailey walks out of the dressing room in her duet pants costume.

"And now for the duet," Miss Donna says. She looks around. "Where's Hilary?"

Bailey shrugs, "Haven't seen her in a while and she's not answering her cell phone."

Miss Donna looks at her watch. "She should be here by now. Only fifteen minutes until you're on." She continues to look around.

Hilary struts up from another direction in her bikini top and Daisy Duke shorts.

"You cut your pants?" Bailey gasps.

The others spin around and see her trashy outfit.

"Why did you do that?" Bailey asks.

"I told you this was the new costume," Hilary declares.

"I'm not wearing a bikini top."

Miss Donna's face turns red.

"Where is your hip hop top, Hilary?"

"I lost it." She lies. "I think my mom might have thrown it away. It kinda looked like a boy's shirt so she probably tossed it by accident. Whoops."

Miss Donna holds her breath.

Avelyn and Kelsi elbow each other. Miss Donna looks like she might explode. Sabine even steps back.

"And why did you cut your pants?"

"They tore so I thought this would be more fashionable," Hilary explains. "Don't you think?" She turns and shows off the ultra-short booty shorts.

"You cannot compete in that outfit!" Miss Donna screams.

"But..." Hilary starts.

"No!" Miss Donna yells.

Hilary stomps off, huffing and puffing like a toddler throwing a tantrum.

Bailey starts to cry, "What am I gonna do? I can't do a duet solo."

Avelyn's face brightens.

"I know the dance."

Bailey looks up from her tear-stained hands.

"You do?"

Avelyn nods. Bailey looks her up and down.

"But you don't have a costume."

"I think we can handle that," Avelyn says.

* * * * * * * * * * * * * * * * * *

Bailey does a breakdance move on the stage. Avelyn slides on the floor behind her. The two jump to their feet and begin a funky foot sequence together. The energy they bring is contagious. The girls in the audience clap along to the music.

"That old costume worked out well," Kelsi says to Miss Donna.

"Just a few modifications," She replies. "Not bad at all."

Avelyn is dressed in a black unitard with a tee shirt over and some accessories. Although the girls look slightly different, their costumes are uniform enough to look believable and good together on stage.

"Maybe Av should replace Hil at all the competitions," Kelsi jokes. "Look at them."

They C-walk and step like pros. As they bow and walk off the stage, big smiles come across both girls' faces.

"That was so much fun," Avelyn says.

"I couldn't have done it without you," Bailey says. "Thanks."

"No problem. That's what friends are for," Avelyn opens her mouth wide. "I'm parched. I'm gonna get a drink. Want something?"

Bailey shakes her head. "Thanks though."

Avelyn walks off.

Bailey walks toward Miss Donna and the other girls. They're all smiles and clap for her. Hilary is nowhere to be seen.

A real friend wouldn't walk out on you, would she?

* * * * * * * * * * * * * * * * * *

Miss Donna taps her toe furiously.

Shawna walks up. Miss Donna looks at her waiting for an answer. Shawna shakes her head.

"Still?"

She looks around and sighs, "Fine. We'll just do it without her. The lines and formations will just need to be tweaked. Let's spread out and take it from the beginning of jazz."

The girls spread out.

"Walk through it."

The girls start to walk through the steps casually moving their arms and changing formations.

Miss Donna puts her hand up, "Stop."

She points to an open space in a line.

"Bailey fill in there, and Shawna move to your left."

The girls move their positions.

"Continue."

The girls resume walking through the dance. Miss Donna points to another spot, "Sabine move in."

Sabine moves into a hole and continues the dance.

The moms talk at the back of the room as the girls continue.

"This is ridiculous. She's got to be around her somewhere," Mrs. Behm says. "Where are her parents anyways?!"

The other moms nod.

"Who wants to look for her with me?"

"I'll go," Mrs. Howser says. "There's no way I'm letting that little brat ruin my girl's medal chances."

A couple other moms follow and head off in search of Hilary.

* * * * * * * * * * * * * * * * * *

The girls are onstage doing the jazz routine. The moms return just in time and stand in the back of the audience to watch. Mrs. Behm holds Hilary back.

The girls do well. Bailey and Avelyn both move into the same pose at the end. They quickly look at one another knowing someone made a mistake, but try to cover and smile at the judges.

"Ha. They messed it up," Hilary says snottily."

"No thanks to you," Mrs. Howser reminds her.

Miss Donna walks toward the group of moms and Hilary. She glares at Hilary.

"Found her," Mrs. Behm says.

"Where was she?" Miss Donna asks.

"Hiding out in her room watching MTV."

Miss Donna glares at Hilary.

"I convinced the maid to let me in. I said it was a medical emergency," Mrs. Behm adds.

"MTV, huh? Bet your parents would love to hear that," Miss Donna says.

"My mom doesn't..." Hilary starts.

"Get changed for the next dance right now, or I'll kick you not only off the team, but out of the studio."

Startled, Hilary suddenly bursts into tears and runs toward the dressing room.

* * * * * * * * * * * * * * * * * *

Hilary gets dressed in her acro costume. She looks over at Bailey. Bailey turns her back to Hilary. Hilary continues to cry.

No one's ever talked to me like that. No one's ever cared enough.

* * * * * * * * * * * * * * * * * *

Hilary isn't her usual self on stage. She is shy and reserved. While she still completes all the moves correctly, she lacks energy and pizzazz.

No one likes me. Not even my mom. Moms are supposed to like you. They're like genetically engineered to like you.

As the girls leave the stage after the tumbling routine, Bailey looks at Hilary, and then begins to talk to Cecilia instead. Hilary mopes.

I wonder if she'll ever talk to me again.

* * * * * * * * * * * * * * * * * *

"And the winners are Nuevo East Dance Company." The MC announces.

A group of boys and girls rush up to him and jump around.

The LDT studio girls sit in a small clump on stage and look

disappointed.

"We didn't even place," Kim groans.

"We sucked," Denver says.

"We didn't suck. They were just better. They were professional!" Cecilia says realistically.

A couple girls nod.

"At least Kelsi's solo did well," Bailey says.

"And Avelyn's," Kelsi adds.

Kelsi looks at Sabine. She is distant and sits on the outskirts of the clump just staring off into the audience.

It wasn't the best for any of us, really.

CHAPTER 15: TRUTH

"This next one counts. The goal is to make it to Orlando Nationals. We'll go to Co Dance Hollywood. We blew the Pulse," Miss Donna addresses the girls who all sit on the wood dance studio floor. "I can't lie that I was more than a bit disappointed last weekend."

A couple girls' foreheads scrunch up wondering why.

"Yes, it was a very competitive group of dancers. Many were extremely talented. But I also feel, you girls, didn't step up to the plate as much as what was needed. And you lost your teamwork. Remember everyone, there is no 'I' in team."

Hilary drops her head.

"That is why I'm setting up five mandatory hours of cleaning and polishing for rehearsal.

A couple of girls moan.

"Beginning right now. Up on your feet."

The girls rise to their feet and shake out their legs.

"Let's start with lyrical."

Bailey and Hilary walk up to one another. Bailey glares at Hilary. Bailey then wraps her arms around Hilary for the opening pose. Miss Donna notices and sighs.

* * * * * * * * * * * * * * * * * *

The girls all wipe off their faces with towels, sweatshirts or tissues.

"Good work today, ladies."

Bailey walks toward her dance bag on the side of the room. Hilary looks at her then turns the other way.

"Bailey and Hilary," Miss Donna says.

They both turn and look at her.

"I'd like a word with you."

The girls each sigh and slowly walk over to her. Miss Donna watches and waits for the other girls to leave.

"So…how's the duet coming?" She asks coyly.

They each shrug.

"Okay, let's get to the point. I don't know what's going on with you two either as friends, or partners, but I do know this: We have a competition this weekend and, like it or not, your duet is entered. It's already paid for, printed in the programs, done," Miss Donna says.

Bailey and Hilary refuse to look at one another.

"So, can we do the duet….together? As a team?" she asks.

"Do we have a costume?" Bailey asks. She bobs her head around at Hilary showing off an attitude.

"I'm sorry, okay!" Hilary yells.

Bailey's face goes blank.

"I know what I did was wrong. I shouldn't have left you there like that. But come on, Miss Donna. Can't we change the costumes a little? They're something my grandma would wear to church," Hilary whines.

"We can agree on something," Bailey whispers

Hilary smiles.

"But it most certainly will not involve bikini tops…or bottoms," Miss Donna says.

"Agreed," Bailey says quickly.

They both look at Hilary. She rolls her eyes a little, "Agreed."

"Good. Now you two go on, and be best friends again, or whatever."

They look at each other, unsure. Hilary wants to say something, but holds her tongue. Bailey is indifferent.

"You did really better without me, I heard," Hilary says.

"Yeah, it was alright," she replies. Bailey looks around the room avoiding eye contact. "Av's got great timing, amazing extensions, she's funny. She never disappoints me."

Hilary looks down, disappointed in herself.

Bailey looks at her, "But she's got nothing on your hip hop style."

Hilary looks up and smirks. Bailey smiles at her.

"Best friends again?" she asks.

"I'd like that," Hilary says.

They smile and walk out of the room talking together.

* * * * * * * * * * * * * * * * * * *

In the hallway, a few girls mingle as they put their shoes away in dance bags or fluff their hair. Avelyn and Kelsi chat together.

"Ice cream?" Kelsi asks.

"I was thinking that yogurt place," Avelyn says.

"Oh, good call."

Sabine sits at the end of the hallway, by herself. She looks sad.

"Should we ask Sabine?" Kelsi questions.

"Yeah, why not," Avelyn says.

Kelsi walks over to Sabine. She jumps when Kelsi touches her shoulder.

"Oh, you scared me."

"Oh, sorry. Av and I are gonna go over to TCBY, wanna join?" Kelsi asks.

Sabine shakes her head, "No, I shouldn't. That's probably not a good idea."

"Okay. Maybe next time," Kelsi says. She walks back over to Avelyn.

Sabine watches her, then turns away again. She grabs her knees, pulls them into her chest, and rocks on the floor. Avelyn and Kelsi grab their dance bags and start to walk out. Sabine watches them turn the hallway corner. She jumps up and runs after them.

"Wait up, I'm coming!"

* * * * * * * * * * * * * * * * * * *

Avelyn devours her cup of frozen yogurt while Kelsi takes slow bites.

"Slow down, killer. You're gonna get brain freeze," Kelsi warns.

Sabine's cup of frozen yogurt sits on the table untouched.

"Aren't you gonna eat it?" Avelyn asks.

"Yeah, if you don't hurry Av might demolish it," Kelsi jokes.

"Have you ever done something you think might be wrong but aren't sure?" Sabine asks.

The girls look confused.

"I always steal my cousin's Wii games even though I shouldn't," Avelyn says. "But I eventually give them back so I don't know if that counts."

"Why what's up?" Kelsi asks.

"You know the dances at the conventions."

The girls nod.

"Like how I've been really good with them."

The girls nod, but more slowly this time, as they try to figure out what she is getting at.

"Like I had them perfect."

"Like you already knew them." Kelsi says.

Sabine stops. "Yeah," she stares at Kelsi for a moment knowing Kelsi knows something. "I did."

The girls both look at her and draw a blank.

"I already knew the dances."

"But how?" Avelyn asks.

"My mom. She registered to be a teacher so she could go and videotape the dances the week before. Then I'd have a full week to practice so I was perfect. That's against the rules, probably? I'm gonna be thrown out and banned from the conventions," Sabine says.

"I don't think it's against the rules. Doesn't seem like it would be. Just frowned upon probably," Kelsi says.

"I'll help you guys. I have the dances for next week and I'm sure I'll get the ones for finals. You can come over and I'll teach you," Sabine offers.

Avelyn and Kelsi look at each other. They both shake their heads.

"No thanks," Kelsi says.

"It's fine that you do it, we're not going to tell on you or anything," Avelyn explains.

"But we kinda like just learning it with everyone else. It's a challenge," Kelsi says.

"That's what makes it a competition. At least that's what I think," Avelyn adds.

She yawns.

"It's only seven o'clock, Kelsi says.

"I can't help it. I haven't been sleeping," Avelyn says.

"Thanks guys," Sabine digs her spoon in the frozen yogurt cup. "Feels good to tell someone what's been going on."

"Honestly…" Kelsi starts.

"We suspected something," Avelyn finishes.

"Really?" Sabine says, surprised.

"Not to put you down or anything but you've never been that good," Avelyn says.

"That quick she means," Kelsi recovers. "You've never picked up choreography that fast."

Sabine thinks for a second. She sways back and forth, "You're right."

Avelyn yawns again.

"Okay, I gotta go, I'm tired."

She stands up and leaves, waving to the girls as she walks away to meet her mom seated at another table.

Sabine turns to Kelsi.

"Thanks."

"For what?"

"Listening."

"Anytime."

Sabine starts to enjoy her frozen yogurt.

"It's really cool hanging with you."

* * * * * * * * * * * * * * * * * * *

Avelyn sits in class. She starts to nod off, then jerks upright, awake. The teacher turns around and faces the board. She starts to nod off again. This time, the teacher turns and spots her. The teacher shakes her head and writes a note on a piece of paper.

* * * * * * * * * * * * * * * * * * *

The phone rings. Mrs. Behm chops a tomato in the kitchen. She wipes her hands on her apron and picks up the telephone.

"Hello?"

Mrs. Behm listens.

"Yes…yes…"

Mrs. Behm's eyebrows lift and her eyes widen.

"Oh, she has, has she?"

She continues to listen, one hand on her hip.

"I'll take care of this for sure…yes…yes…thank you for your time."

Mrs. Behm hangs up the phone.

Oh, Avelyn!

* * * * * * * * * * * * * * * * * *

Mrs. Behm drives. Avelyn sits in the passenger's seat.

"Your guidance counselor called today."

"Oh," Avelyn says.

"Apparently, you've been falling asleep a lot in class."

"I've just been tired."

"And falling behind on your studies, a couple of teachers commented." Mrs. Behm continues.

Avelyn is silent.

"Anything to say for yourself?"

Her eyes fill and she bites at her lip before speaking. "I should have said something sooner. Something is wrong with me. I'd like to see a doctor."

"For what?" her mom says alarmed.

"To help me sleep. I can't make my mind shut down and I hardly sleep at all at night. But then, I am sleepy all day. I don't remember the last time I wasn't tired."

"Avelyn, if your studies don't improve, you'll have to cut back on dance. School is the priority you know. You just have to get more rest."

"I know."

Mrs. Behm recomposes her posture. "We'll just start getting you to bed earlier." They sit in awkward silence and Avelyn stares out the window.

"So, everyone excited this weekend? Lots of pressure. Have to place well to get to nationals," Mrs. Behm nearly sings, her discomfort clear.

"I want sleeping medicine. This is really serious. I can't sleep. Like insomnia. "

"Honestly, Avelyn."

"Mom," Avelyn looks directly at her and irritation creeps into her tone. "I need sleeping pills. I have been trying to sleep since September and it's not working!"

"Okay, honey. We'll take care of it. I promise. I will talk to our doctor and see what she suggests."

Avelyn looks ahead and looks faintly happy.

Ah...sleep.

CHAPTER 16: TREMAINE

The girls stand around in a circle and jump. They stare at the stack of trophies in the center of the circle.

"We did it, we did it!" they sing together.

"Going to nationals!" Molly yells.

The girls put their hands in, then lift them up in the air and dance around. The parents stand back and laugh as the girls go wild.

"All the solos will be going to nationals, as well as the duet!" Miss Donna announces.

Sabine, Kelsi, and Avelyn jump with excitement. Bailey and Hilary hug each other.

Avelyn runs over to her mom and hugs her.

"You were amazing, darling."

Avelyn beams with pride.

Mrs. Behm examines the ribbon wrapped around Avelyn's wrist. It reads "Crowd Pleaser."

"It really was."

"Thanks," Avelyn says as she yawns.

"Oh, and I talked to the doctor. She recommended you take this. It will help you to fall asleep," Mrs. Behm pulls a small vitamin supplement type bottle out of her purse. "It's melatonin, all natural to help you fall asleep. And if that doesn't work I have a list of other things to try starting with removing stress from your life."

Avelyn looks at it and smiles.

"Thanks. I really do need this. And I was stressed about dance this year, more than ever."

"I know. But you did great."
They hug once more.

CHAPTER 17: CO DANCE NATIONALS

The group is at class, learning a jazz routine. It's fairly simple, just stylized. Avelyn and Denver really get into the moves. They giggle as the instructor shakes his booty to the floor. Sabine struggles. She can't seem to remember the dance and misses steps.

"Break it up!" The Nancy O'Meara yells. The girls and guys break up into smaller groups. She points to one group. Kim, Abby and Kelsi take the floor amongst several other dancers. Kelsi stands out instantly with her perfect kick, straight to the head. On the side, Sabine tries to mark the dance and still forgets which way to turn after the double pirouette and kick across step.

The next group takes the floor. Avelyn watches Sabine from across the dance floor. Sabine continues to follow along with those dancing on the floor. She seems lost.

Avelyn elbows Harmony, "See that?"

"What?"

Avelyn points to Sabine, "Sabine."

"Yeah, so, she's marking the dance."

Avelyn shakes her head, "Never mind."

"Next group!" The teacher yells.

Sabine takes the floor. She looks nervous. She finds a place near the back.

The music starts. She's a mess. She has some of the moves, but she lacks confidence and does make several mistakes.

The teacher points to several dancers; Sabine is not one of them. She walks off the dance floor hanging her head.

I didn't make it. I've never not made the first cut.

Avelyn and Kelsi both notice.

"She's never not made the first cut," Kelsi says.

"I know," Avelyn agrees.

"I thought she was getting all the dances ahead of time."

"Apparently, not this time."

Sabine watches as all her friends continue to move on.

Gosh dangit, mom! I can't believe she convinced me to do this all season. I can't believe I went along with it. Now I'm so behind. I don't even remember how to remember a dance anymore.

She looks confused.

Wait, is that even possible? To not remember, how to remember?

She shakes her head.

Get your act together, tap is next.

* * * * * * * * * * * * * * * * * * *

Sabine sits on the floor with Kelsi and Naomi. The girls tie their shoes.

"I can't believe I made it to the final round," Naomi says. "I've never made it to the final cut."

Kelsi smiles, "You were good."

Sabine concentrates on tying her laces perfectly. She takes deep breaths.

Forget about everything before. Just tap.

Gregg, the instructor, is on stage with his assistants. Kelsi looks up at the stage, as she ties her second shoe.

Gisela taps around casually on stage marking a number.

Zel? Kelsi thinks.

Gisela laughs. It's a big, silly laugh. Kelsi smiles.

Zel!

She jumps to her feet and runs over to the stage.

"What's she doing?" Naomi asks.

"Who knows?" Sabine says.

"Zel," Kelsi says happily.

Gisela turns and see Kelsi. She freezes for a moment and studies her face.

"Kelsi?"

Kelsi nods.

Gisela smiles. She hops down from the stage. Kelsi gives her a hug.

"What are you doing here?" Gisela asks.

"Hello? Competition girl," Kelsi says, mocking herself.

"Not the Kels I remember from last summer. She turned into a ballet bunhead for sure."

"Yeah, tell me about it. I just can't make up my mind!" Kelsi sighs. "So, what are you up to? Tapping with Gregg Russell? Pretty nice gig."

"I'm just helping him for the day," Gisela explains. "I've been at NYCB all year."

"Really? No tap?"

"I'm trying to get my mom to see the real me. But I don't know. I really want to tap with Gregg all summer and take classes with him next year...well if he invited me, of course."

"Wow. That would be incredible!"

"Tell me about it." She nods. "How 'bout you? What adventures have you been on this year?"

"Just back at my old studio." Kelsi shrugs. "I mean it's great but I think I'm gonna audition for New York again. Ballet's actually my love, and I don't get very much here. I have to do my own barre before class each day."

"So, we converted you then," Gisela says with a wink.

"And you're being converted yourself as well, wouldn't you say?"

"Yeah, yeah."

"Zel, we need to do a run through," another assistant on stage says.

"Yeah, be right there."

Kelsi smiles, jealous.

"I gotta go. But we'll stay in touch, right?"

"Of course," Kelsi says.

"Message me."

"Will do."

They hug. Gisela waves as she runs up the stairs to the stage. Kelsi watches her in a happy daze.

I miss New York.

CHAPTER 18: FINALE

A large sign outside an auditorium reads "National Finals." Several girls, guys, and their parents come in and out of the venue. Inside, the girls are dressed in their animal print acro costumes. Molly kicks up to a handstand and her feet touch a wall. She holds the position. Harmony stands by and coaches her.

"Now do ten," she says.

Molly bends her arms and does a push up in the handstand position. "One."

Molly continues and Harmony counts.

"Two, three."

Denver and Shawna practice a lift with Cecilia, where she is suspended in the air on one leg while in an arabesque penchée. The lift is incredible.

Avelyn stands at the back of the room. Sabine and Kelsi stand on opposite sides of each other to create a clear runway area for tumbling. Kelsi nods. Avelyn points one foot forward, takes a deep breath then runs and lunges into a round-off back-handspring back tuck, jump spin and down into the middle splits. She stands up, satisfied.

"How'd that one feel?" Abby asks.

"Good. Ready."

* * * * * * * * * * * * * * * * * *

The girls perform the routine on stage. Everything looks great. The costume and music create an eerie and wild feeling. The tumbling sequences pop out of nowhere making them appear like animals in attack mode. And the cool lighting effects work so well with the music that they feel like they are in Cirque.

The routine ends with Avelyn's big tumbling pass coming forward. She jumps into her middle splits and stares intensely at the judges.

* * * * * * * * * * * * * * * * * * *

Kim, Abby, and Naomi smile and swing their hair around as they chaîné and spin into axel jumps. They move to the sides and Harmony, Cecilia, Sabine, Kelsi, Bailey, and Avelyn spread out for a turn combination. Harmony concentrates hard.

Prep and double.

Bailey smiles.

Fouetté, fouetté, and out, out.

Avelyn is confident.

Double, change spot, fouetté.

Cecilia focuses on her plie.

Plie into the spot change. Okay, fouetté. Double, plie into the spot change.

She does a double and changes her spot to left side of the stage.

Got it. One more.

The girls all do a double pirouette, then change spot to the front again and do three more fouetté turns. Everyone smiles. Miss Donna sits in the audience and holds her breath. The girls complete a triple pirouette and finish right foot back, arms up. Miss Donna breathes a sigh of relief, then claps.

The girls spin out of the pose into the next moves. Sabine rolls over her ankle as she spins. Her face clenches in pain, and she opens her mouth wide to yell, but nothing comes out. She chaînés to the side and hobbles out of the way.

Sabine immediately begins to cry. The girls continue on with the dance. Kelsi sees Sabine on the side.

"You okay?" Kelsi asks as she looks back and forth between the stage and Sabine.

Sabine shakes her head. She has her leg lifted and touches her ankle. Kelsi looks back to the stage, "Be right back."

Kelsi jumps onto the stage and continues the dance with everyone. They strike their pose and then everyone rushes to the side to exit. Kelsi runs to Sabine.

"Av," she calls and nods to Sabine. "Help me."

Avelyn rushes over and helps Kelsi lift Sabine. They carry her down the stairs. Sabine continues to cry.

The other girls follow, concerned. Avelyn and Kelsi carry her over to Miss Donna.

Miss Donna's eyes are wide.

"What happened?"

"I don't know. I just saw her on the side crying," Kelsi says.

"She rushed off after the turn combination when she was supposed to go into the rotating kicks," Denver says.

"Put her down," Miss Donna says.

Kelsi and Avelyn carefully lower her to the ground.

"I...I..." Sabine tries to speak. The tears and pain prevent her from being clear.

"I rolled over my ankle," She finally manages.

Mrs. Howser rushes over.

"What's going on here?"

Sabine looks up at her, tears still flood her eyes.

"I hurt my ankle."

"Hurt your ankle?" Mrs. Howser repeats.

Sabine nods.

"Does it hurt here?" Miss Donna asks as she carefully pushes on Sabine's ankle.

Sabine nods.

"How about here?"

She presses on another spot.

Sabine shakes her head, "No."

"How about here?"

"Ooowwww!" she cries as she jumps.

Miss Donna slowly lifts Sabine's leg a couple inches off the ground. "Anything?"

Sabine shakes her head.

Miss Donna places Sabine's leg and foot back on the floor.

"I think she sprained her ankle," Miss Donna says to Mrs. Howser.

"Sprained her ankle? Oh, that's nothing. Good then."

"Mrs. Howser, a sprained ankle is painful. Especially the first day." She looks at Sabine. "I'm sorry but I'm afraid you'll have to sit out the rest of the routines."

Sabine nods through tears.

"She will not be missing her dances," Mrs. Howser says. "I'll simply wrap it up, and she'll be good to go. Right, Sabine?"

Sabine stares, unsure how to respond.

"I'm afraid I can't let you do that. As the owner of the studio, I am allowed to determine who is ready to dance and who isn't."

"But we've already paid all the fees. You can't tell us we can't dance now."

"When it's in the best interest of the child I can." Miss Donna defends.

"She still has her solo to perform. She can at least do that," Mrs. Howser fights. "You want to do your solo, don't you Sabine?"

Sabine weakly nods though she is still crying.

"Naomi, go ask the lady over there for a bag of ice," Miss Donna directs.

Naomi rushes over to the concession.

"Mrs. Howser, I cannot stress how important this is. If she dances on her ankle the way it is right now she can make it worse. We don't even know if it's just a sprain. It could be a fracture or a torn ligament. Continuing to put extreme pressure on it with dance can even cause permanent damage. Is one solo in her life really worth that?"

Mrs. Howser glares at her.

"I'm going to tape it up and she'll be fine. Period," Mrs. Howser says.

Naomi returns with a bag of ice.

"Thanks, Naomi, " Miss Donna lays the bag on Sabine's foot. "Hold it here for at least twenty minutes and keep your foot elevated on the chair." Miss Donna looks at the rest of the girls gathered around. "The rest of you go on and change for tap. The show must go on."

Mrs. Howser walks away out of ear shot as she talks on her cell phone. Miss Donna looks Sabine in the eyes. "I really don't want you to do your solo. I always want to see you dance, just not like this. Please don't go out there. You'll just be in pain."

Sabine swallows hard. Her tears are almost gone. She looks over at her mom and then at Miss Donna, unsure what to do.

* * * * * * * * * * * * * * * * * * *

The girls tap away on stage. Sabine watches from the audience. Her ankle is wrapped with medical gauze. The tap is on. Everyone is full of energy and the taps themselves sound amazing. The dancers finish with a final stomp. There's a moment of silence, then the audience erupts in applause. Everyone, even the judges stand and clap. The girls giggle with delight then leave the stage quickly.

Sabine wipes away a single tear.

I should have been up there.

* * * * * * * * * * * * * * * * * * *

Kelsi has headphones on and an IPod in her hand. She marks through her solo. Avelyn does the same, singing to herself as she dances. Sabine watches and cries. Denver and Shawna sit with her.

"It's alright," Shawna says.

"Yeah, I know it sucks but it's for the best," Denver adds.

"Easy for you to say. I've worked all year for this. All year. And now, now I feel like it was all a waste of time. All the practices and stretching and eating healthy. All of it. For what? For nothing," Sabine cries.

Mrs. Howser stands at the back of the audience on her cell phone. "I said immediately!" she yells into the phone. "No dear, it's not an emergency. She's fine. She's going on for her solo. She'll be just fine...don't tell me what to do...she's being a whiner. It was nothing...I was here I should know."

Miss Donna walks over to Sabine.

"How are you feeling?"

Sabine shrugs through tears.

"Sure you don't want an Advil?"

"I'll take one if you still have it."

Miss Donna reaches into her purse and pulls out a small bottle of Advil.

"One or two?"

"One." She overhears her mother in the background yell, "She's a superstar." "Make it two."

"Shawna, can Sabine have a sip of your water?"

"Oh, yeah, cool." Shawna hands Sabine a water bottle. She takes down the Advil in a jiffy.

Mrs. Howser marches over.

"Sabine, why aren't you dressed yet? You go on in ten minutes."

Sabine starts to sit upright and attempt to stand. Miss Donna places her hand on Sabine's thigh.

"You don't have to do this. It's your body. You can make a choice."

Mrs. Howser pushes Miss Donna's hand away and jerks Sabine's arm pulling her up. Sabine winces in pain from the sudden movement.

"Don't you dare touch my daughter. Sabine, once competitions are done we are changing studios." She glares at Miss Donna. "Touch her again and I'll slap you with a harassment suit."

Mrs. Howser starts to walk away with Sabine who limps and grimaces.

"Sabine!" Miss Donna yells.

Sabine stops and turns around.

"Do you want to do your solo right now?"

Sabine thinks hard. She looks at Miss Donna, then at her mom. She shakes her head side-to-side.

"No."

"What?" Mrs. Howser screams.

"I don't want to do it. My ankle hurts too much. I'll just look foolish." Sabine explains.

"Why are you doing this?" Mrs. Howser asks.

"What?"

"I can't believe you're doing this to me. After all I've done for you. All the private lessons, all the fancy costumes, all the taped performances so you could get an edge on the competition."

The other girls' eyes widen in shock.

"You little snot."

Sabine's face goes blank. She doesn't know what to do.

Did my mom just say that? Am I really a little snot?

"Mom..."

"Don't mom me. I'm done. I'm done, done, done," Mrs. Howser walks away.

Sabine breaks into tears. Miss Donna and a couple of the girls go to comfort her.

Miss Donna wraps her arms around her. "It's okay, she's just upset. You're doing what's best. You made the right choice."

"How come the right choice feels so wrong?" Sabine asks.

Miss Donna rubs her back. "It's not your fault."

Kim, Abby and Harmony watch from afar.

"Poor Sab," Abby says. "She can't do her solo."

"And her mom was really mean," Harmony adds.

"I know, she was all like 'it's all about me' and stuff," Kim says.

"That just sucks."

"Totally."

"Agreed."

They all stand with their arms crossed and sigh at the same time, as they watch Sabine continue to cry.

* * * * * * * * * * * * * * * * * *

Kelsi sits on the stage, dressed in her solo costume amongst several other girls including Avelyn. She crosses her fingers and closes her eyes. Avelyn holds her hand and looks up at Barry Youngblood who is about to announce the winners.

"And the champion, to be crowned top soloist of the national finals is…Kelsi Little!"

Avelyn screams,"Ahhhhhh!" She squeezes Kelsi's hand and mauls her with a hug.

Kelsi smiles, excited but not overwhelmed with craziness like Avelyn. She walks up to the front of the stage. Barry's assitant brings up a huge trophy, nearly as tall as her. Kelsi lifts it up.

"It's pretty heavy," Barry says.

"That's alright," Kelsi replies.

She lifts it up over head.

This is supposed to be it. This is supposed to "the" moment. Why don't I feel like a superstar?

She continues to smile as a million thoughts go through her head.

This isn't where I belong anymore. I'm going back to New York. I'll get in again for summer, I'm sure. I don't know where I'll end up, but that is where I need to train.

She stares out in the audience at her friends and family.

After the summer, I'm staying. I'll work my butt off to be asked to stay. I'll be in New York for high school in the fall. I can do it. I can do anything!

Avelyn stands at the back of the stage and claps, all smiles.

She deserves this. She worked harder than anyone else. I'm sorry for being jealous, Kelsi. The truth is…I want to be like you…good job, Kelsi. I'm so proud!

Out in the audience Gregg Russell looks around. He spots Sabine sitting on a chair, leg up. He looks at her foot.

"Oh, no, what happened?" he asks.

Sabine sits up quickly, surprised to see him.

"What? Oh, it was just a little something…rolled over my ankle,"

She answers.

"Well, hopefully that heals quickly 'cause I wanted to invite you to my summer intensive."

"Your summer intensive?"

"Yeah, I noticed what a good tapper you were yesterday, and I think you'd be a great fit for the summer program. That is, if you'd want to come."

Sabine's face lights up. "Want to come? I'd kill to come!"

"Awesome. Here's my email." He hands her a business card. "Shoot me an email, and I'll send you the details."

Sabine looks at the business card in shock and awe.

"Thank you. Thank you so much." She tries to stand up to hug him but struggles.

"Don't. Let that heal. I'll see you in the summer."

He waves and starts to walk off.

"See you in the summer!" she calls.

She smiles from ear to ear.

Gregg wants me to come to his summer intensive. Ahhhhhhhh! Yippee!

CHAPTER 19: CHEERS

Miss Donna holds a glass and raises it in the air to a huge table with all the girls and their parents. "To a surprising," she looks at Hilary who blushes and holds onto Bailey, "an incredible," she looks at Sabine and Avelyn, "and well-deserved year" she looks at Kelsi. Everyone else clinks glasses.

"And on that note, I'd just like to recap the high points of national finals." She picks up a piece of paper and begins to read: "Out of three national competitions we traveled to three different states, won 12 group awards, 2 overall solo awards and several others. It was amazing and I am so proud of all of you." Miss Donna sits down. Everyone begins to talk amongst themselves.

"Enjoy this dinner, it's the last time you'll see these friends," Mrs. Howser says to Sabine.

"What? What are you talking about?"

"I'm switching studios for you. I thought I already made that clear. I talked to Joanie the other day and she said Michelle's school, that Dance Institute Works, is pretty good. I don't know, we'll try it out and see. If we don't like it, we can always find somewhere else. Or I could just get you a private coach."

Sabine's jaw nearly hits the table. "I'm not going somewhere else."

"It's already done. You're not coming back here."

"Switch studios and I'll stop dancing."

Mrs. Howser actually looks her in the eyes.

"You heard me. I'll stop. I'll never dance again," Sabine says seriously.

"You wouldn't do that."

"Yes I will. Here's the plan, mom. I'm going to let my ankle heal and then I'll start back at Miss Donna's. And…I'm going to a tap intensive over summer."

Mrs. Howser is now the one with the dropped jaw and look of shock.

"Oh, yeah, and it's in New York," Sabine adds. She cuts her piece of chicken and happily eats it.

At another table, Avelyn bites at her nails and struggles to look at her mother. "Mom," Avelyn says tentatively. "I think I want to cut back next year."

"Really? Why sweetheart?" Mrs. Behm asks.

"I love dance. I really do. But I want to focus on school more. I was so stressed this year and I was so tired and, well I think I might be interested in psychology. Figuring out how people think and stuff."

"Wow," Mrs. Behm says. "Whatever you want, darling. You're a smart girl. You know how to make good choices." She smiles and winks.

"Thanks."

That wasn't so hard. And I feel relaxed. And relieved.

Hilary and Bailey share a bowl of pasta.

"I can't wait till rehearsal next year. I'm going to practice every day," Hilary says.

"Sounds good. Hard work is the way to go," Bailey agrees.

"Hey, wonder if we'll get a duet again next year."

Bailey pauses and thinks, "Maybe solos would be a better idea."

They both smile and laugh.

Kelsi watches all the action at the table and gently smiles.

It's been good here. But I'm ready for something else. New York, here I come!

CHAPTER 20: NEW CHAPTER

A sign on the door of an industrial building reads "NYCB Auditions."
Kelsi comes out of the door, a big smile on her face. Amanda waits
outside.

"So?" she asks.

"What do you think?" Kelsi asks.

Amanda cautiously nods.

Kelsi nods back.

Amanda throws her arms around Kelsi's neck and hugs her.

"Automatic acceptance," Kelsi says.

"Oh, I'm so proud of you," Amanda says.

A beep sound and song are heard. Kelsi pulls her cell phone out of
her dance bag.

"I have a text," she says.

She opens up her phone..."From Sabine."

She reads the message to herself.

*Doctor cleared me to dance. Headed to the tap intensive. Do you think your
friend Gisela will be there? Hope you got in. Miss you!*

Kelsi smiles.

*Her adventure is about to begin. And mine...mine is....heading into a new
chapter.*

ABOUT THE AUTHOR

In addition to Dance Divas, Airin Emery has written six other books in the Dance Series, by Lechner Syndications. After a professional dance career that included everything from Fosse to Cirque du Soliel she has changed gears and now focuses her artistry on choreography and writing. She maintains co-ownership of a dance studio in the Midwest, adjudicates for competitions & festivals and currently lives in Malibu with her husband, three children, and two precocious dogs.

Made in the USA
Middletown, DE
03 December 2015